"Will you marry me, Angel?" Chris said, holding her in a grip of steel. "I want to love and take care of you always."

And the love Diana saw in his eyes tore at her heart. It was so deep and sincere that for a moment she had to look away. Was she sure she wanted Chris? For a lifetime? It would be so wrong if she were leading him on, even unintentionally.

DOROTHY LEIGH ABEL has an insatiable appetite for life and has expressed many of her own experiences in her novels. Though involved in many activities, Dorothy feels the most totally alive when she is actively creating a story.

The Tender Melody

Dorothy Leigh Abel

HARVEST HOUSE PUBLISHERS
Eugene, Oregon 97402

In memory of
E.A.P.
whose beautiful gospel songs
inspired this story

THE TENDER MELODY

Copyright © 1984 by Dorothy Leigh Abel
Published by Harvest House Publishers
Eugene, Oregon 97402

ISBN 0-89081-428-7

Printed in the United States of America.

"My Singing Is A Prayer"

My singing is a prayer, O Lord, A prayer of thanks and
    praise;
In music, Lord, I worship thee; Thy beauty fills my days.
I give my talents, Lord, to thee, My mind and heart and
    voice,
For thou alone art worthy, Lord; In thee I do rejoice;

Accept the worship of my heart, Accept my music, too.
Help me to live always for thee, Lord, keep me strong and
    true.
O, bless me, Lord, and help me sing Thy love so full and
    free;
And bless all those who listen, Lord, Help them to worship
    thee.

Chapter One _____

"Won't you have another piece of birthday cake, Aunt Vi?" Diana asked, standing to slice another piece from the platter.

"Where on earth would I put it, child?"

"The same place you put the last piece!" retorted Beth, one of the slender teenagers at the table for her second piece.

"I think I'll take my cup of coffee into the living room," the middle-aged woman announced with determination, "and remove myself from this immediate area of temptation."

Before she carried her ample frame from the room, Diana's eyes met hers across the table. Diana's sister Cindy had finished her piece of cake and left the kitchen for the adjoining living room. She was sitting on the loveseat by the front door staring out—unseeing, unmoving—as though all the cares of the world had been hurled upon her slim shoulders.

Was Aunt Vi thinking as she was, Diana wondered, that Cindy's birthday party had reached a bit of a lull?

It had begun cheerfully, with Cindy's two best friends, Beth and Corey, joining in with Diana and Aunt Vi.

Mr. Denny would have come too, but now...

Diana had been reluctant at first to have the party, afraid that it would have the opposite effect from the one intended, that it would bring back painful memories. Of course it would, Aunt Vi had told her niece. Nothing could keep away the memory of the accident that took place a year ago this day. But it was, after all, Cindy's thirteenth birthday. It was a significant time in a girl's young life when she officially became a teenager. Had circumstances been different, Cindy would have shrieked with delight at the idea of a get-together with her friends—all of them.

Diana glanced at her watch, deciding it was time.

Corey and Beth, already informed of what would happen next, joined Diana and Aunt Vi in the living room.

"Cindy, come on, honey," Diana urged, taking her sister by the hands and pulling her gently to her feet. "We have a surprise for you."

Cindy stared unseeing at the group around her. "Another surprise?"

"Oh, the party was only part of it," said Beth.

"Yeah," Corey added with an appealing grin, "the best is yet to come."

"But I've already opened my presents. Even what Mom and Dad sent."

"I have a little something else for you," Diana said. To Cindy's look of amazement, she added, "You have to go with me to get it." She smiled conspiratorially at Aunt Vi and the girls.

"Why do I have to go with you? You want me to try it on or something? Is it another blouse?"

"You'll see," Diana said, a jubilant tone in her voice.

"What kinda surprise is it, Diana?" Cindy asked. "You sound like you can't keep it a secret much longer."

"I can't. Now come on, let's go," she said, tugging her sister along toward the door. "We don't want to be late."

A dusky sky of cloud swirls tinted rainbow colors by the sunset hovered peacefully on the horizon as the little group strolled along Briar Court to the intersection of Franklin Highway and Langford Road three blocks away. It was a calm, still evening in late August, the heat of the day receding in welcome relief with the setting sun as they passed lovely brick and stone houses nestled amid gracious lawns of shady trees and resplendent flower beds.

As they strolled along, Diana remembered the evening a year ago—the car accident, the race to the hospital, the doctor's words. She would never forget the doctor's words, "Even a tiny sliver of steel is capable of making an eye completely and irreparably blind if it strikes with enough momentum to penetrate the anterior wall, the iris, the lens and vitreous, and finally lodges in the retina."

As a result of the accident, her sister had been irretrievably blinded in both her eyes. This party was to help bring Cindy out of her depression. Even though the entire family had been deeply scarred by the tragedy, their feelings could be nothing compared to what Cindy suffered.

What must it be like to wake up one morning from a world of light and life to face a world forever dark and gray? Where do you begin to make the adjustment to such a shock and grief, especially when you were a lovely Christian girl with a lifetime stretching before you?

Adjusting hadn't been easy for Diana either. But she was a gallant young woman who had already fought more than one battle in her twenty-one years. Just six months before Cindy's accident, Diana's fiance had summarily called off their engagement.

She sighed deeply at the remembrance. It had been difficult, but Diana had spunk and strong faith. She had forged ahead with plans to keep the furniture she and her fiance had bought and moved into the apartment they would have shared as husband and wife. It had taken courage for her to leave her longtime home in Aunt Vi's apartment to set up housekeeping on her own with Cindy. But Diana was of age now and wanted to be more independent.

And it was only natural that Cindy preferred to live with her sister, the girls having always been close in spite of the difference in their ages. The absence of their parents, far away serving the Lord in Bangladesh, had encouraged their closeness. Diana and Cindy were girls of strong character; the foundation for which had been laid down before they came to live with Aunt Vi in Briar Ridge, a pleasant suburb of the mid-Southern city of Briarton. But their widowed aunt had done her part by keeping them on the Christian path. She had kept them involved in church and related activities, doing her best to rear them along with her son in a wholesome, loving atmosphere.

Diana felt confident that God would see them through. He had already helped her mend the pain of the broken engagement, and someday she would trust again, someday she would love anew. *Maybe*. And God would help Cindy too, even though after a year's time she still seemed deeply hurt, unnaturally bitter. The loss of sight was a devastating crisis, something like losing a loved one, Cindy's teacher had said, but to a girl who had become a Christian only weeks before, the grief must seem too overwhelming.

Perhaps the plans she had for Cindy tonight would brighten the girl's dark life, if only for a short while.

Returning to the present, Diana guided the entourage from the residential section to a side street. They exited near the side entrance to the new Briar Ridge Auditorium.

The auditorium of cream-colored brick stood sleek and modern in the fading sunlight. Surrounded by spacious parking, the front of the building was long alternating panels of brick and darkly stained windows, with the roof extending forward and supported by dark brown columns to create an open loggia.

Inside, the lobby was roomy and thickly carpeted with an enclosed box office. The lobby was crowded with people moving toward the doors on the right that led into the large auditorium.

"I know where we are," Cindy said smugly. She stood to one side of the ticket office, between Beth and Corey. "I've never been here before," she went on to tell them, "but I know we're at the new auditorium. I even remember what the outside looks like. It was finished you know before...before..."

Diana glanced quickly at her sister. The innocent and delicate beauty she saw in her face wrenched at her heart. Everything had been going so well. The party, instead of reminding Cindy of the accident as she had feared, had seemed to lighten her spirits, until a short while ago. But now...

Diana flicked a glance at her watch. Only fifteen minutes until the concert. Fifteen minutes and everything would be all right again!

Looking into the crowd, Diana recognized Art Ross, owner of the auditorium, conversing with her aunt. He and his wife had been friends of Aunt Vi's since before her husband died. It was Mr. Ross who had helped Diana make this such a special night for Cindy. A slightly-built man of medium height with thin, grayish hair, he approached Cindy and her friends, then wished the girl happy birthday, and thrust a small package into her hand.

He greeted Diana with a warm handshake and a welcome smile. "I carried out your instructions to the letter, Diana," he said softly.

"I can't wait to see the expression on Cindy's face when she hears them. She doesn't have any idea why we're here."

"She'll know soon," Mr. Ross said, glancing at his watch with a hurried gesture. "I have seats for all of you down front. You'd better get seated. It's almost time."

Art Ross led the way across the lobby to the main double doors that opened into the auditorium. Down the wide center aisle he came to a stop at the third row of seats.

"How's this?" he asked, turning back to look at Diana.

"Wonderful, Mr. Ross. I can't thank you enough for all you've done."

Aunt Vi took a seat along the row and Cindy and her friends followed. Diana stood for a moment in the aisle with Mr. Ross.

"I talked to Christopher Jarrett two weeks ago," he said confidentially. "He was glad to do what you asked."

"Two weeks ago! Oh, Mr. Ross, what if he forgets? I mean, it will be a thrill for Cindy anyway, but if...well, it will be so much more special for her if he remembers."

"Relax, Diana," he said, reaching out to squeeze her hand. "I talked to him a few minutes ago backstage in his dressing room. He hadn't forgotten my call."

"Oh, Mr. Ross, I'm so excited!"

"You better sit down now. They'll be starting the concert any minute."

Diana slid into the seat next to her sister as Art Ross took off along the aisle, smiling and greeting people as he went.

Immediately Cindy assailed her sister with questions. "What's going on, Diana? Why did you bring me here? Nobody will tell me anything."

Diana wouldn't either. She only sat confidently, smiling a smile Cindy couldn't see.

Chapter Two _____

"What were you and Mr. Ross talking about?" Cindy queried into her sister's stubborn silence.

It was silly to be so excited, Diana told herself. Cindy and she had grown up on old-time gospel quartet music. Aunt Vi had taken them to countless concerts at local churches and auditoriums. They had even gone to one all-night gospel sing in Atlanta several years ago. Year before last they had gone with Aunt Vi to the Gospel Quartet Convention in Nashville. That's where Cindy had fallen in love—with The Jarretts Quartet—and Christopher Jarrett in particular.

Oh, they had heard his group before then. Cindy and she had all their albums except the latest one, but Cindy had been still a little girl in many ways until recently. Now she seemed almost as grown-up as her sister. But if she were more grown-up than she had been two years ago, she was still occupied with her first big schoolgirl crush. This crush had taken form in one Christopher Jarrett, manager and lead singer of the famous quartet.

"Diana, did we come to see a play?" Cindy persisted.

When Diana assured her they had not, Cindy said on an exasperated note, "Well, what *did* we come to see?"

Diana scanned the length of the stage before them. Four microphones were in position at the front. To one side a piano sat at an angle. At the back of the stage were a set of drums and in front of them three stools for the other musicians.

A guitar leaned against each stool. At each end of the stage stood giant amplifiers. For a moment Diana wondered if the sound wouldn't be deafening at such close range. But the incredible softness of Christopher Jarrett's baritone couldn't be offensive at the peak of the amplifier's volume, she decided.

"We came to listen," Diana said at last.

"Listen to what?" Cindy wanted to know.

As if that had been the cue, lights dimmed and the announcer, a short, heavyset man, walked across the stage to one of the microphones. The auditorium grew suddenly quiet.

"Ladies and gentlemen, welcome to Briar Ridge Auditorium. It is my great pleasure tonight to introduce to you gospel music's favorite quartet, three-time winners of the Fan Awards at the Gospel Quartet Convention in Nashville. Ladies and gentlemen, Briarton's own—The Jarretts Quartet—featuring the magnificent voice of your favorite lead singer—Christopher Jarrett!"

The announcer left the stage to a generous applause as five men in matching brown slacks and tan blazers walked quietly on stage. One man sat down at the piano, another behind the drums, and the other three took places at the tall stools, picking up their guitars as they were seated.

In the next minute an even more gentle hush fell over the room. On the bright stage four men strolled casually to the microphones. They were dressed alike in dark brown suits and creamy white shirts.

When Christopher Jarrett spoke, Diana faced her sister. She was staring in shocked disbelief toward the stage.

"Let not your heart be troubled," the quartet's lead singer quoted. "Ye believe in God, believe also in me. In my Father's house are many mansions..."

The musicians began to play then and the quartet's splendid harmony filled the quiet room:

In my Father's house are many mansions,
If it were not true He would have told me so;
He has gone away to live in that bright city,
He's preparing me a mansion there I know.

Then the lead singer sang in his golden voice:

Jesus died upon the cross to bear my sorrow,
Freely died that souls like you might have new life;
But I know there soon will come a bright tomorrow,
When the world will all be free from sin and strife.

A tall, lean man with dark hair and mustache let his deep
voice float out over the room:

Do not shun the Savior's love, from up in glory,
Or you won't be there to sing the gospel story;

The entire quartet concluded:

In my Father's house are many mansions,
If you're true then to this land you'll surely go.

Cindy, her face aglow with delight, said to her sister, "Oh,
Diana..., Diana..." But that was all she could utter, for
Christopher Jarrett was speaking again.

"Good evening, ladies and gentlemen. As the announcer told
you, we are The Jarretts." He turned to the man on his left.
"This is my cousin, Billy, who sings high tenor for us. On my
right," he said with a gesture, "is Uncle Don, our second tenor.
To my far right is the newest member of our group, our bass
singer, taking my daddy's place, Malcolm Clayton. I'm Chris
Jarrett. I sing lead for the group." After introducing the musicians, Chris Jarrett said again, "We are The Jarretts. And we
love to sing and play for Jesus. You know why?"

The quartet blended their voices:

Because...He touched me and—made—me whole...

At the conclusion of this song, the lead singer said, "Before
we go any further and before I forget, we'd like to dedicate
this next song to a very special young lady." His gaze took in
the portion of the audience immediately in front of the stage,
which laid in the shadow of the bright lights.

"*Cindy*, wherever you are—Happy Birthday to you, Happy
Birthday to you—Come on, everybody—Happy Birthday—

God Bless You—Happy Birthday to you!''

Chris Jarrett smiled. "Cindy, a little bird told me the name of your favorite gospel song. It just so happens it's one of our favorites too. We'd like to sing it for you now."

The quartet was little more than halfway through their wonderful version of "Peace in the Valley" when Diana felt a teardrop splash onto her cheek. She couldn't look at Cindy, too overcome was she by the joy she knew her sister was experiencing. It had been long months since a man had stirred anything even resembling a pleasant emotion in Diana, but Christopher Jarrett had come close. It was kind of him to make Cindy's birthday surprise so special, and while it could never make up for the tragedy that had occurred a year ago this night, Diana realized it went a long way in cheering Cindy out of her recent grief and depression.

When Diana felt her sister's hand on her arm she turned. The girl's face was a picture of shining loveliness. What she would give to keep that look of happiness there. But it seemed only Christopher Jarrett was capable of doing that. At intermission she must find a way to thank him. He would be overwhelmed with fans and autograph seekers, but if she waited patiently maybe she would get her chance. Of course, Cindy would refuse to leave until she, too, met her favorite singer and acquired his autograph.

"So this was your surprise," Cindy whispered, throwing her slender arms around her sister's neck and giving her a bone-crushing hug. Beside Cindy, Diana glimpsed Beth, Corey, and Aunt Vi smiling in their direction.

"How did you do it?" Cindy asked in a minute.

"When Mr. Ross told Aunt Vi that The Jarretts were going to give a concert here at the auditorium, I planned right away that we would come. When I found out they would be here on your birthday, I couldn't believe the coincidence."

But maybe it wasn't such a coincidence after all, Diana thought, recalling the event surrounding Cindy's accident.

"Did *you* talk to Chris Jarrett?" Cindy asked excitedly.

"Oh, no. Mr. Ross spoke to him. He told him it was your

birthday and asked him if they'd sing something special for you."

And what a time she had, Diana added silently, keeping Cindy's friends from mentioning the upcoming concert and spoiling the surprise.

"Ladies and gentlemen, we'd like to thank you for coming out to hear us sing tonight," Christopher Jarrett was saying. "We hope you've heard something that lifted your spirits and made you feel closer to the Lord. In a few minutes we're going to take a short break, and if you'd like to get one of our albums they'll be on sale out in the lobby."

At intermission the quartet left the stage to resounding applause, and Diana glanced at her watch as lights flooded the auditorium. Had forty-five minutes gone by already?

"Diana, can I go out in the lobby and get his autograph?" asked Cindy.

"I don't think so," Diana said mischievously. "What do you want his old autograph for?"

"Oh, don't tease me!" cried Cindy. "Let's hurry or we'll never get near him."

Diana watched the throngs of people spilling into the aisles and moving quickly toward the exits to the lobby. "We probably won't anyway. Let's wait till after the concert. They'll still be selling their records then, and maybe we'll have a better chance to meet Mr. Jarrett."

The second half of the concert went on for more than an hour. It seemed the quartet didn't want to stop singing and the time sped by with one song after another of Southern gospel favorites—"An Evening Prayer," "Mansion Over the Hilltop," "Bosom of Abraham," "Swing Low Sweet Chariot," "Working on the Building." The last song was a special arrangement by the quartet's lead singer to bring out not only the harmony of the group, but, with individual microphones, emphasized his baritone and the high tenor's voice simultaneously, as well as the addition of the bass singer's deep tones.

In the lobby Diana and her little group approached a long table stacked with record albums. The four men who made up the singing voices of The Jarretts Quartet were standing behind the table, laughing and talking and signing albums for many people.

Aunt Vi turned to Diana as they waited in line at one side of the table, "I think I'll take Beth and Corey on home," she said. "It's going to be awhile before Cindy gets to meet Mr. Jarrett."

After Cindy's friends said good-bye, Aunt Vi started across the lobby with them and Diana turned back to the task at hand. From where she stood at Cindy's side she could see her sister's still-radiant glow. *If only she could be like this again,* thought Diana. *If only she could accept what happened, as difficult as that was.* But tomorrow she would be feeling sorry for herself again and blaming God for her accident and still hating Mr. Denny.

Dear Lord, Diana prayed in her heart, *I know I've asked You countless times to help Cindy, and I know she's not responding to You. But please don't give up on her. Please, God!*

It was then that a break came in the crowd around the table and Diana tugged her sister forward so that the two of them were standing face-to-face with Christopher Jarrett.

He gave Diana the sweetly intimate smile that was such a part of his natural charm and made all women fall in love with him at once. All of them, that is, who hadn't already fallen hard for the sound of his magnificent voice. But Diana had been innoculated against the effects of handsome, charming men like Christopher Jarrett. Or so she imagined. And believing that she was immune, the only feeling he prompted in her, even at such close, stirring range, was one of profound gratitude.

"Mr. Jarrett," she began, "my name is Diana Jansen, and this is my sister Cindy."

Christopher Jarrett was a moment in acknowledging her introduction as he turned to greet Cindy. Diana had noticed he had been watching her approach from some distance away, and she couldn't help wondering what he was thinking, a man of his striking appearance and high regard. She had been told that she was pretty, but not in the usual sense of the word. She had large, happy eyes, green with little flecks of gold, and her chestnut-colored hair hung in silky strands over her shoulders. But her appeal was more in the way she moved, friends had said, something almost regal in the way she held herself. She was barely average height, but she seemed so vital, so alive and ready to meet the challenges of life.

"It's a pleasure to make your acquaintance, Cindy," Chris replied in a soft, Southern drawl.

"Thank you for singing to me tonight," she said.

Chris glanced at the white cane she held nervously between clenched fingers. "I always enjoy singing to beautiful young ladies," he said.

Her sister *was* beautiful, Diana thought. Her face was exquisitely wrought and shining and she was slender as Diana herself was. She had almost the same flowing tresses and her eyes were a lovely deep blue. Now Cindy faced Chris with a faint blush and timid smile so becoming to her.

"I hope you have many, many more happy birthdays, Cindy." He picked up a record album from a stack nearby. "Will you let me give you a little gift?" he asked and touched her hands with the record. "This is our latest album."

"Oh, thank you, Mr. Jarrett. I don't know what to say."

"Mr. Jarrett," Diana said, "I wanted to thank you for making Cindy's birthday a time she'll never forget. And now this." She paused, flicking a glance at the record. "I don't know what to say either."

"You've thanked me. That's more than enough."

"Mr. Jarrett, would you sign your name on the album for me?" Cindy said. "Sign it by your picture. Your picture is on the album, isn't it?"

"Yes. We're all on there."

"I know I can't see your name," Cindy went on, "but knowing it's there will be okay. I can feel where you write it."

Chris glanced at Diana. Her expression was tender and sorrowful.

Carefully the singer tore the cellophane wrapping from the album, then signed his name on the cover above his head in the photograph of the quartet sprawled across the front. "I'll get the other guys to autograph it for you, too," he said.

Diana watched him stride away to the other end of the table with an easy grace that sprang from a natural confidence in himself, she thought, from an assurance born of knowing his right place in God's will and without overrating his own merit.

Chris returned in a few minutes and gave the album back to Cindy. Diana and she thanked him again for his kindness, then turned and started across the lobby. The group of people around the table had thinned considerably, and Diana had gone only a few steps but still she wasn't certain if she heard her name being called in that familiar Southern drawl.

When she stopped and looked over her shoulder, Christopher Jarrett was smiling at her. "Come back here a minute," he beckoned softly. His smile was one of the nicest things about him, one of many nice things, she decided.

After a slight hesitation, Diana left Cindy and returned to the table. When she did it became obvious that Chris Jarrett was at a temporary loss for words. But he looked down on her with a warmth in his eyes that told her more than any words could have. And it wasn't that he hadn't seemed kind, he had been exceptionally so. And if appealing good looks could turn her head, Christopher Jarrett wouldn't have found it necessary to call her back to the table. But the truth was Diana wasn't interested in the singer, or any other man, no matter how nice or how handsome. Not even his benevolence to Cindy could penetrate her well-placed armor.

"I...uh...." Suddenly he picked up a record at random from one of the stacks on the table. "Here," he said, thrusting it into her unwilling hands. "I gave Cindy one, I'd like to give you one, too."

Diana recognized his offer for what it was—an awkward attempt to get better acquainted with her. If circumstances had been different, she might have been tempted. But she was still so afraid.

"It isn't my birthday," she said, without even a smile to soften the abruptness of her reply. Glancing at the album as she placed it back on the table, she added, "Anyway, I already have this one."

He laughed. "All right. I confess. I was just trying to—"

Chris paused and Diana flicked her gaze to the man who came up beside him. He was the man the singer had introduced onstage as his cousin, Billy.

She smiled pleasantly at him before turning back to the group's lead singer with a determined look in her green eyes. "Good-bye, Mr. Jarrett. It was nice meeting you."

She left the table and when she reached Cindy waiting nearby, she hurried her across the lobby toward the front door.

"She didn't sound like meeting you was very nice," Billy said.

"I guess I insulted her," said Chris. "It's been so long I must be out of practice in striking up an acquaintance with a woman."

"Why don't you go after her and apologize," Billy replied. He regarded his cousin thoughtfully for a minute. "If you're interested. If I'm any judge, you look like you're interested."

In two hasty strides Chris was around the table. "I am."

"She's probably got a stag line three miles long," Billy tossed after his cousin in good humor.

"I'll get in line then," Chris threw back over his shoulder.

"Maybe she's married!"

"If she is, she doesn't wear a ring," Chris said to no one in particular as he weaved around a few last-minute autograph seekers on his way to the door.

Diana and Cindy were stepping from the front loggia into the parking lot when he caught up to them. At the sound of her name, Diana whirled around, staring at him in speechless amazement.

Chapter Three _____

"Hi," Chris said. "I'm sorry if I made you angry back there."

"Mr. Jarrett!" Cindy exclaimed.

"Hello again," he said to the girl, placing a gentle hand on her shoulder.

"You didn't make me angry, Mr. Jarrett," Diana said.

"My name is Christopher. But if that's too much, try Chris."

So Christopher Jarrett was the persistent kind, thought Diana. *Well, so was she. Persistent about not being pursued. Not now. Not after...*

"We've already said good-bye," Diana told him firmly.

"I just thought I could...uh...see you to your car."

Cindy giggled. "You'd have to see us home to do that."

Chris looked at Diana. "You live near here?"

"Yeah," Cindy answered before Diana could speak. "It's only three blocks."

He smiled. "May I walk you ladies home?"

"That's awful nice of you Mr.—Chris," said Cindy.

Diana frowned and said, "Thank you, but we'll be fine. We're used to walking."

In the lighted parking lot Chris looked down on them from his considerable height. "It's really dark this late. I'd like to see you home." Diana started to protest but he forestalled her with, "Which way do we go?"

Their eyes clashed and held in a battle of wills. In a minute

Diana could see that their unwanted escort wasn't about to be talked out of seeing them safely to their apartment. Obviously the handsome young singer intended to become friends with them. *Well, why fight him after all?* Even if she didn't care to get to know him, it would be a thrill for Cindy to get acquainted with her current singing idol.

"This way," she said at last and started across the nearly deserted parking lot toward Langford Road.

They had crossed the street and turned onto Briar Court when Cindy said, "Mr. Jarrett, when—"

"Chris."

"Oh, yeah. Chris, when will you be singing in Briar Ridge again?"

"As a matter-of-fact, we'll be back at the auditorium two weeks from tomorrow night."

"At the Saturday night Old-Time Gospel Sing they're gonna start having?"

"They'll be having it twice a month. We're booked for quite a few of them."

"I guess you must be awful busy," Cindy said.

"We cover a lot of territory," Chris replied. "We've been to so many towns I can't remember their names."

"It must be exciting going so many places."

"I suppose if you've seen one town, you've seen them all, what we get to see of them. But you meet a lot of interesting people." He glanced sideways at Diana, but she walked solemnly along, apparently content to let Cindy and him carry the burden of conversation.

And so he talked on and on with his young admirer until Diana slowed to a stop before a two-story brick building. "This is where we live," she told the singer.

In the light pouring down from the street lamps Chris gazed at the building with its dark roof and rows of white shuttered windows. A brick walkway led through a velvet lawn up to a long, columned porch where baskets spilling over with Boston fern hung between the white columns. Flanking each side of the wide front door, also painted white, were two enormous emerald philodendrons. Beneath each of the four windows on the first floor sat smaller pots of pandanus (cornstalk plant) and asparagus fern and baskets of Swedish ivy.

"This is a nice place," Chris said. "Somebody sure likes plants."

Diana felt Cindy stiffen beside her. "Aunt Vi is very fond of them." *And so was Mr. Denny.*

"Your aunt lives here, too?"

"She owns this building and the one next to it."

Chris flicked a glance at the other brick building, identical to the one in front of him.

"Thanks for seeing us home," Cindy said to him.

"It was my pleasure, honey."

The girl's blind eyes reached toward the singer. "Would you like to come upstairs and have a piece of my birthday cake, Chris? Aunt Vi made it. My favorite. Chocolate fudge."

Chris studied Diana. The expression on her face made him feel anything but welcome. But when he glanced at Cindy again, the hope and expectation on her shining features sent a pang through his heart.

"I'd really like to, Cindy, but I can't tonight. I left the guys to do all the loading up at the auditorium. Maybe I could come another time real soon."

"Oh, would you?" Cindy said, offering him a bright, tender smile. "I'll save a piece of cake just for you."

"I'll be back. I promise," Chris said and cast a lingering gaze at Diana.

"I guess I'd better go on upstairs now," Cindy said. "Good night, Chris."

"Good night, honey," he said, and with her slender cane Cindy made a low arc in front of her as she went along the walk and into the apartment building.

"I'll say good night too," Diana said.

"Must you go?"

She stared up into his handsome face, a wary look in the depths of her gaze. "Yes."

"May I ask you something first?" When she made no reply

but looked up solemnly at him, he said, "What caused Cindy's blindness?"

"She was in a car accident. It was a year ago...a year ago tonight."

Diana didn't tell the singer the rest of what that meant—that similar to tonight Cindy had been on her way to hear his quartet sing at a concert in a nearby town. She sensed that if he knew, although he could in no way be blamed for what happened, still he might feel unnecessary remorse.

"That's why I was especially grateful for what you did tonight," she continued. "Cindy has been a special fan of yours for quite a while now and tonight you helped make her forget the accident."

"I'm glad I could do something." He paused. "I'm so sorry Cindy's blind. She's a beautiful little girl."

"It's hard to believe that her face was pretty badly scarred right after the accident. The plastic surgery worked miracles." She smiled up at him then. "I really have to go now. Thank you for walking us home."

Chris grinned beautifully. "You're welcome, *Miss* Diana Jansen. It is 'Miss,' isn't it?"

"Yes," she answered slowly. And then to herself—*but I'm not interested in you, Mister!*

When she started up the walkway, Chris gazed thoughtfully after her. As she disappeared inside the building, he turned and strode off along the sidewalk. Diana had no way of knowing he would have to take some kidding from the guys when he got back to the auditorium. Billy would tell them that the last time he saw Chris he was chasing after some young woman. And he would add that it was about time Chris got interested in someone again.

•   •   •

Upstairs in the apartment Cindy was in the kitchen cleaning up after the party when Diana came in. The girl was singing to herself as she worked. *How wonderful to see her happy—and helpful—again,* thought Diana, *if only temporarily, and even if she had Chris Jarrett to thank for it.*

"You don't have to bother with that tonight," Diana said. "We can do it in the morning before church."

Cindy was at the sink, her arms emerged in sudsy water. "Is Chris gone?" she said, ignoring her sister's statement as she came up behind her.

"Yes."

"Imagine him singing to me," Cindy sighed. "And walking us home, too. He's sure nice, ain't he?"

"*Isn't* he?" Diana moved to a row of cabinets beside the sink. She took a fresh towel from a drawer beneath the counter. "Yes, he seems very nice."

"You don't like him, do you?"

Diana picked up a wet dish with a sigh of resignation. It had been this way since the accident. She could keep nothing from Cindy. Every inflection of her voice told the blind girl more than any words would. "I don't even know him."

"Would you like to get to know him?"

"No."

"But he's so nice. And he sings like an angel. What's he look like?" she added on a wistful note.

"Don't you remember?"

"It's been almost two years since we saw him in Nashville. Anyway, that was at a distance."

"But you've seen his photograph on all their records hundreds of times."

"It's been a year since I've seen his picture. I've forgotten a little. Describe him to me. He's tall, I remember."

"He's about 6'1'', I guess. He's got shoulders like a football quaterback, without the shoulder pads." Cindy giggled as Diana went on, "He's got a lean, muscled build and his hair is sort of light brown, a honey-brown I guess you'd call it."

"How does he wear it?"

"It's blown back softly away from his face."

"Describe his face."

"His forehead is wide and his cheekbones are far apart. He might have some Indian blood in his background somewhere.

His nose is narrow and straight and his chin is square." *And determined,* she added silently, *like "the" man.*

Cindy faced her sister. "You took a lot of notice of him, didn't you?"

"Well... I notice things. People. Maybe it's that little bit of the artist in my nature."

"You notice what's beautiful, especially."

"Oh, Chris isn't exactly beautiful, not even in the male sense."

"Yes, he is. He's real handsome. I remember that even if I don't recall the details. But the part of him that's really beautiful isn't the part you can see with your eyes."

Diana stared at her sister. She had always been quick, intuitive, and comprehending for her age. But she seemed even more so now. Somehow she had an uncanny way of seeing right inside a person, of going right to the center of what a person actually was, like aiming an arrow at an unsuspecting target. She could see qualities that sighted people often missed, the qualities that truly mattered, Diana tacked on thoughtfully.

"You just don't like Chris," Cindy was saying. "That's why you can't see what he really is." When Diana made no comment, Cindy said, "You didn't tell me what color his eyes are. You don't have to. I'll never forget how blue they are."

Diana gazed past her sister at some imagined object across the room. *Chris Jarrett's eyes were blue,* she mused, *the bluest blue she had ever seen.*

• • •

Diana dressed for church Sunday morning in a white eyelet dress. It had a square neckline, full, short sleeves and a three-tiered skirt ending in a lace hem. The dress gave her appearance a fresh, country-summer look. She wore a simple gold chain around her neck and had on white high-heeled sandals. Cindy wore a bright yellow dress with matching sandals. As the girls strolled side by side down Briar Court to the church, the morning sunlight splashed on the peaceful suburban scene and caught the red and gold tints in Diana's and Cindy's long curls.

"I hate to leave you by yourself this afternoon," Diana was saying, "but it's my Sunday to work."

"Oh, that's all right," said Cindy. "I'll find something to do."

Diana glanced briefly at her as they stopped for traffic at the corner. That same joyful note of last night was still in her voice. Bless Chris Jarrett's heart! Now if only he would keep his promise to come back and have cake with Cindy soon, for she knew this hope of a visit from the popular singer was responsible for the rise in her sister's spirits. But realizing how busy The Jarretts were and understanding that their lead singer had already done more for Cindy than anyone had a right to expect, Diana thought it best if she was prepared to face possible disappointment in any further gestures from him.

"You and Aunt Vi can do something this afternoon. Or maybe Beth and Corey will come over."

"Maybe. But I don't really want to do anything. I hope they don't come."

If Cindy had spoken this way even two days ago, Diana would have had no doubt about the cause. She had lost interest in nearly everything since her blindness. No matter how hard she and Aunt Vi tried, they couldn't cheer Cindy for very long. Not even Cindy's closest friends could help much. But because Chris Jarrett had shown some interest in the girl , she was riding high on a wave of expectation, probably hoping that his promised visit would come this very afternoon.

Diana remembered then that the members of The Jarretts Quartet lived in or near Briarton, and she began to wonder in sincerity if Chris Jarrett would recall his seemingly casual words to a blind girl who innocently adored him.

Chapter Four _____

Cindy sat on the loveseat in the living room her thoughts fixed on nothing. From the stereo across the room the beautiful harmony of The Jarretts Quartet filled the air. When she had played a stack of their records through two times, she put on an album by a well-known gospel singer. A lively version of "Jesus Will Outshine Them All" had finished playing when she heard someone coming up the hall stairs, taking them two steps at a time. In a minute the buzzer sounded at the door. Cindy went to turn off the stereo. At the door she paused with her hand on the knob.

"Who is it?"

"It's Chris Jarrett, Cindy."

She turned the lock and yanked the door wide open. "I knew you'd come!" she cried, thrusting a tender, innocent smile toward his face. Mirrored in her expression was all her hope and trust and adoration of him, and Chris felt almost ashamed that the primary reason for his visit was to see Diana, not her little sister. "I really didn't think you'd come this soon, though," Cindy finished.

"We sang at a local church this morning," Chris said, "at an anniversary service. We sing again at the service there tonight, but I'm free this afternoon."

"Well, come on in," Cindy said, stepping back, then closing the door behind him.

In the living room Chris glanced around. On the wall to his

left was a broad window that looked out on the street below. Cream-colored priscilla-style curtains hung at the window. A damask-covered couch in a green floral pattern was positioned beneath it with matching loveseat occupying the wall by the door. Creamy white tables holding tall lamps sat at each end of the couch and a large table in an octagon shape nestled between the couch and loveseat. A beautiful potted plant was centered on the low coffee table. Just inside the door, next to the loveseat, stood another leafy plant that reached more than halfway to the ceiling. Across the pale carpet a long stereo console filled the wall.

Chris turned his gaze toward the kitchen, which opened in full view off to the right of the living room. Wooden cabinets and gleaming appliances were arranged in a convenient U-shape, and in the middle of the tiled floor sat a round table and four chairs. Decorating the table was another potted plant. It bore clusters of white, star-shaped flowers among its waxy, oval leaves and emitted the sweet fragrance lingering in the apartment.

Chris strode with an easy confidence over to the couch and took a seat. Cindy sank onto the cushions of the loveseat, her blind eyes reaching toward him.

"What's that stuff you're wearing?" she asked. "You had it on last night, too. It sure smells nice."

He laughed softly. "It's *Brut*."

Cindy giggled. "But you're not a brute, Chris." She stood up suddenly. "Would you like a piece of cake now? I saved it for you like I said."

He smiled across at her charming graciousness, though he knew she couldn't see. And he surmised, after another glance around, that her even more charming sister wasn't at home this afternoon.

From where he sat on the couch Chris watched Cindy at the kitchen sink filling a porcelain kettle with water. "You'd like a cup of coffee with your cake, wouldn't you?"

"Yes, a cup of coffee would be nice."

"Do you use cream and sugar?" she asked, setting the kettle

on the front burner of the electric range and reaching for the corresponding button to turn it on.

"I take it black."

At a cabinet near the sink Cindy reached up and took out a china cup and saucer and a small plate. She felt into another cabinet and brought out a flat, plastic container. When she had placed a large piece of chocolate cake on the plate and carried it to the table and put a napkin beside it, Chris got up and joined her.

"You want some ice cream?" she asked when he had settled his lean, wide-shouldered frame in a chair across from her.

"Sure. What's cake without ice cream?"

Cindy stood by the range for a minute, overcome with smiling joy, at being in Chris Jarrett's presence, at his actually being in *her* apartment, in *her* kitchen, about to eat a piece of *her* birthday cake. Oh, he was really nice, nicer even than she had imagined him to be! She only hoped...

But, she didn't dare ask. Maybe she didn't truly want to know. Not yet. If he had come today only because he pitied her, because she was blind and supposedly helpless, how that would hurt. Why did everyone think that anyway? Well, nearly everyone it seemed. It was so easy to tell the difference between those who considered her an equal person—like Diana and Aunt Vi and Corey and Beth—and those who didn't know how to relate to her or who made her feel inferior.

Cindy couldn't tell about Chris Jarrett yet. He didn't appear to be uncomfortable with her, but she hardly knew what he was really like. Oh, she could sense how genuine he was, but she hadn't learned his personality. How she hoped he wouldn't begin treating her in a well-meaning but condescending manner. That would hurt just too much!

When Cindy returned to the table she brought Chris a bowl of ice cream and a fork and spoon. She could sense he watched her at the range, measuring instant coffee in the china cup. She carried the cup and saucer to the table and went back for the hot water ready in the kettle.

When she had filled the cup to about one-quarter inch below

the rim, he said, "How do you know when the cup is full?"

"They taught me at school to put my first finger just inside the cup to feel the heat." She took the kettle back to the range and then sat down opposite her guest. "I used to burn my finger at first. I'd pour too fast and it would splash out."

"I suppose you learned real fast that way."

"I sure did."

"Do you attend the state school for the blind in Briarton?"

"Yes. We started back this week. I catch the bus in front of the shopping center. It drops me off a block from the school."

They were silent for a few minutes then, while Chris drank his coffee and worked on the cake and ice cream. When he finished he took his dishes to the sink.

"Thank you, Cindy. That was very good."

"Do you want some more coffee?"

"I still have some."

"Why don't you take it into the living room? That's what Diana does."

Chris smiled at her again. "Where is Diana this afternoon?"

"It's her Sunday to work. She works at Marshall's over on Langford Road."

Chris was familiar with the large, well-known department store to which Cindy referred, although he didn't often get out to do any shopping there. Perhaps he could find more time for it—now.

"Diana only works part-time. She's studying to be a commercial artist. She goes to college in Briarton. She graduates next spring."

"What does she plan to do then?"

"She wants to get into public relations work. At the seminary if she can. But she does a lot of drawing now for our church. And she does publicity for Mr. Ross at the new auditorium. Sometimes she does ads for Marshall's. She did that picture of me in the living room."

Chris got up, and taking his coffee cup, went to stand near the door. He was still studying the sketch of Cindy mounted over the loveseat when she came up behind him.

"She did another sketch, too, of our parents. It's in her bedroom."

"Your sister does beautiful work. I'm no judge, but I'd say she's very talented."

"That's what everybody says."

Chris went to the couch and Cindy took the chair beside the stereo. "I guess she takes after Aunt Vi. She likes to draw, too, but she's got a little arthritis now and doesn't do it much anymore."

"So you and Diana live here in your aunt's building. How long have you been here?"

"How'd you know Aunt Vi owns the building?"

"Diana told me last night."

"Oh yeah, that's right. Did she tell you our parents are in Bangladesh? They're missionaries."

"She didn't mention that."

"Aunt Vi is our father's sister. We've lived with her since we started school."

"Your aunt sure must love flowers," Chris said. "The foyer downstairs looks like an ad for a jungle safari."

"Aunt Vi loves plants and flowers, but Mr. Den—"

Cindy broke off and Chris sent her a puzzled look. In a minute when she didn't go on, he glanced around. "What's that big plant over by the door?"

"It's a weeping fig," Cindy answered stiffly.

Chris looked at her again, examining her suddenly stern features reflectively for a time.

"This is a nice plant on the coffee table," he said, his blue gaze taking in the exquisitely flowering plant of red and yellow satin-look blooms.

"That's an achimenes," said Cindy dryly.

"I think I like that thing on the kitchen table best. What's it called?"

"That's an angelwing jasmine," she said and smiled tenderly at him. "It's called the Flower of Romance."

He studied the plant thoughtfully. "An angel of a flower for an angel of a girl," he said before he realized it.

"Cindy, does your sister have a boyfriend?" Chris asked on impulse then.

"No," she replied at once, glad that he'd gotten off the subject of Mr. Denny's plants. She didn't want to talk about them or her aunt's handyman. She didn't want to talk about him ever again. She just wanted to forget he was alive.

"Diana's pretty, ain't she? I mean, *isn't* she?"

"Almost as pretty as you are."

Cindy's radiant cheeks turned bright red. "Thank you. She gave me this blouse," the girl said, plucking nervously at the soft fabric at her neckline. "She got it for my birthday. She was going to buy your new album for me, too, but you gave that to me."

"What time will Diana be home from work?"

"She gets off at six tonight."

He flicked a glance at his watch. It was almost six o'clock now. He could wait for her, but he wouldn't have any time to stay after that. As it was he would barely make the concert tonight.

"Would you like a *Thingamagig** while you're waiting for her?" Cindy said.

"A *what*?" Chris laughed.

"See the box on the coffee table?"

Chris looked down at the box decorated in blue and white squares with darker blue printing across the lid. "Yes."

"Open it."

He lifted the lid and Cindy said. "Those are *Thingamagigs*.* They're caramel and pecan candy. The coating is white chocolate. Mr. Ross gives them to me every year for my birthday. He gets them from somewhere in Texas. You can have some if you want."

Chris replaced the lid. "Thanks. Maybe next time. I'm full of cake and ice cream right now."

---

* Registered trademark. Mary of Puddin Hill, Inc., Greenville, TX.

Next time? Then he must be planning to come back thought Cindy happily. *He wanted to come back to see Diana, naturally. Why else had he been asking so many questions about her?* And he hadn't said anything to the contrary when she mentioned he was waiting for her to get off work. *That's probably why he came in the first place.* She smiled a secret smile.

"Diana likes *Scutterbotches**."

"You're putting me on."

"No, I'm not. Honest. That's what they're called—*Scutterbotches**. They're made out of butterscotch and raisins and peanuts. Mr. Ross gets them at that same place in Texas."

In a few minutes the door opened and Diana walked into the room. Pushing back a lock of chestnut hair, she spotted Chris rising from the couch and a stunned expression swept over her face. Gratitude was the next emotion she felt, because he had remembered his promise to Cindy. But the look on his face told her it wasn't Cindy he was thinking of now.

---

* Registered trademark. Mary of Puddin Hill, Inc., Greenville, TX.

Chapter Five _____

Early the next morning Diana was making a cup of coffee when Cindy came into the kitchen. Both girls were dressed for school.

"Good morning," Diana greeted. "Wearing your new blouse again today, huh?"

When Cindy made no comment, but went to the refrigerator for a glass of milk and sat down quietly at the table, Diana, with her cup of coffee in hand, took the chair next to her. "All right. What is it?"

"You know," Cindy said after a brief hesitation.

"It's last night, isn't it?"

"You weren't very friendly to Chris."

"Cindy, honey, I—"

"I know. You've had one broken heart, you don't want another one."

"Do you blame me?"

"Chris wouldn't break your heart."

Diana smiled fondly at her sister. "You really like him, don't you?"

"I guess he's about the nicest person I know. He doesn't treat me like I'm some terrible kind of freak, but he doesn't act like I'm not blind either. He treats me like he knows I am, but it doesn't matter. He sees me, Cindy, a girl who's blind, not a girl who's blind named Cindy. He sees me first and then my disability."

"Maybe I can be nicer the next time he comes," Diana said on a note of resignation. *How could she discourage the joy in Cindy's voice when she talked about the singer?*

"Imagine him living so close to Briar Ridge," Cindy said brightly then. "Just twelve miles out Franklin Highway, he said, then a mile after you turn off till you get to their farm. I'm surprised we haven't seen him around before. But he said he stays pretty busy singing and helping his dad run the farm. Anyway, he won't have so far to come to see you."

"Cindy—"

"It's you he really came to see yesterday. Doesn't that just make you go all weak and silly inside?"

"No, it doesn't," laughed Diana. "You're the one with the crush on him."

"Yeah, I know. But it's not so much really. He's way too old for me. How old do you think he is anyway?"

"I don't know. About thirty, I guess."

"*That* old?" Cindy said and made a distorted grimace.

Diana laughed again. "*That* should make him feel good."

"I think I just want to be his friend. But I think he wants you to go out with him."

What kind of a complicated situation was she getting into, Diana wondered. *Chris Jarrett was obviously destined to become the personal delight of Cindy's young life, but where did she, Diana, fit into this?* That he was interested in her, she had no doubt, but she didn't have to encourage Cindy along this line of thinking. And if it weren't for Cindy she'd tell him kindly but plainly not to seek them out anymore. Perhaps that's what she should do anyway, before Cindy became too attached to him. He said last night he would call one evening this week. Probably she would be working, but if not she would ask him not to call anymore.

Cindy left to catch her bus, and Diana spent a few minutes tidying the kitchen, then went into her bedroom for her Bible. Back at the kitchen table, she sat down for her morning devotion time. Each morning when Cindy had gone she still had half an hour before she had to leave for her classes and this way of beginning the day, with a prayer and some verses of Scripture, had become a long established habit. It began when she was a small child and lived with her parents. Aunt Vi had continued this family time of shared devotions.

"There's something about starting the day with a prayer," Aunt Vi often said. "It seems the day just goes better, no matter what you have to face."

Cindy had stopped taking time for morning devotions right after the accident.

When Diana picked up her Bible, she began thumbing randomly through the New Testament. At the thirteenth chapter of Hebrews she stopped suddenly.

Let brotherly love continue. Be not forgetful to entertain strangers: for thereby some have entertained angels unawares.

Cindy had said Chris Jarrett could sing like an angel. Diana didn't need anyone to tell her this. He had the most beautiful, expressive singing voice she had ever heard. Even when he talked, his tone was like a gentle melody. *Had God's Spirit led her to these verses for a reason this morning? Was she being hasty in her decision not to go out with him? If he asked her. And he would. So what then? Would he build her hopes and make promises he couldn't keep? Would he...*

Impatiently, Diana forced her thoughts away from the past. No point in dragging all that up. It was ancient history. And she had recovered. Completely. Only the scars remained. And the fear. Fear of ever trusting a man again. Fear of the indescribable, incomparable hurt. Fear of giving away her heart only to have it carelessly tossed back.

Diana closed her Bible. She was assuming a lot. Just because a man asked her to go out didn't mean he would one day ask her to become his wife. Maybe she would go out with Chris, but she wouldn't be good company. How could she be? Then he wouldn't call anymore, he wouldn't come by. And that would be that.

When Cindy came in from school that afternoon, Diana was

at the table in the kitchen again. This time she was working on some layouts for Art Ross. Cindy put on the album Chris had given her and as Diana stared down at the posters she was working on, ads for the Saturday night gospel sing, she thought suddenly how surrounded she seemed by reminders of Cindy's favorite singer. (And yes, her favorite singer, too.) When images of his handsome face floated before her—his sweet, haunting smile, and those blue, blue eyes—distorting the letter she was trying to shape, she threw down her pencil and stood up.

It was that moment when the telephone rang. Cindy went to the little table in the hall to answer it. Relief poured over Diana when she heard Cindy speak Corey's name. *It was relief she felt, wasn't it? She hadn't actually been hoping Chris would call? Of course not!*

It was Thursday evening before Diana got the call she didn't want. While she was at work. Chris chatted with Cindy instead and before he hung up he asked if Diana and she would be at the gospel sing a week from Saturday.

"I'm planning to come, but I don't know if Diana will have to work or not."

She didn't. But at intermission when they went out to the lobby there was such a number of fans gathered around the long table where The Jarretts and other groups sold their records, that they couldn't get anywhere near Chris. When the concert was over and the various quartets that had come to sing began to leave the auditorium there was still so much confusion and so many, many people that they finally gave up on trying to see him.

Cindy was silent as they walked home that night and during the week that followed she resumed much of her former attitude before Chris Jarrett had personally entered her life. She took little notice of what went on around her. She shunned even her two best friends and hardly talked to Diana or their aunt. Only when she sat in the living room playing one of The Jarretts' albums did she appear to have any joy about her.

Had it been a mistake, Diana wondered now, *that special attention from Chris on Cindy's birthday?* But she'd only asked, through Mr. Ross, that he mention her sister's birthday and sing her favorite gospel song. It had been his idea to give Cindy the record and to walk them home. It had been his promise to come for a piece of cake, and to call last week. But he hadn't called this week. He had been too busy no doubt.

• • •

As Diana was leaving for classes Friday morning during the last week of September she met Mr. Denny in the hallway downstairs. He was bent over the bronze wandering jew in the corner by the door to her aunt's apartment. The grace and fullness of the plant as it spilled over its white wire planter seemed to Diana a kind of twisted tribute to all the heartache and sorrow they had suffered the past year. How could so much beauty be representative of so much sadness? The plant had been anything but that when Mr. Denny gave it to Cindy.

Mr. Denny was a gray-haired man in his early sixties. He had a large, portly frame, and could usually be found with a stubble of beard. A belying twinkle of good humor in his gray eyes and an inviting good nature had endeared him to all the residents in Aunt Vi's two apartment buildings. That was until a year ago.

In trade for the apartment across the hall from Diana and Cindy, Mr. Denny was general maintenance man and jack-of-all-trades for their aunt, serving her devotedly day after day for as long as Diana could remember. She wasn't sure but what Mr. Denny hadn't had a romantic interest in the woman who employed him sometime in the distant past. An unusual love for plants and flowers wasn't the only thing these two had in common, but if Aunt Vi looked on the handyman as anything other than a friend, no one knew of it.

Mr. Denny straightened and turned from the wandering jew when he heard Diana's footsteps in the hall behind her. She felt a stab of remorse when her gaze fell on his haggard face. The past year had taken its toll. The lines in his face were deeper, his lips thinner, and in his eyes she saw the sorrow, the regret, the guilt.

"Morning, Mr. Denny," she greeted cheerfully.

"How are you this morning, Diana? I saw Cindy leave a little while ago."

The expression on his face told her that her sister's attitude toward the old man hadn't changed, that she hadn't even spoken to him on her way to school. Diana went over to him and put a comforting arm around his drooping shoulders. "Give her time, Mr. Denny, she's very young."

"I'd give *my* eyes if I could change what happened," he said. "I'd give my life!" he added, almost gasping on the words. "She's got her whole life ahead of her and mine's almost over. It should be already," he said with so much disconsolation that Diana winced.

"That wouldn't change a thing," she said gently. "What happened was an accident. It wasn't even your fault."

"Cindy thinks it was."

Diana had been participating in variations of this same conversation with her aunt's handyman once or twice a week, every week, since that fateful night. She never stopped feeling sorry for the old man, and of course she bore him no grudge, but she didn't know how to begin to ease his pain. Only Cindy could do that, in some measure, for probably he would never completely get over what happened. But Cindy refused to have any more to do with Mr. Denny. Not only that, she'd given back the beautiful wandering jew he'd grown for her birthday the year before last, the lovely plant that had seemed to blossom and grow as a symbol of the special bond of love these two had shared.

Cindy had loved all the flowers and plants in her aunt's apartment building. She had taken a great pride in helping Mr. Denny water and care for them. Now she hated the old man who had become like a grandfather to her and she couldn't tolerate anything remotely connected with him. Not even her prized wandering jew.

It had been a stormy night, that evening last year when Mr. Denny had agreed to drive Cindy over to Belle City to hear The Jarretts in concert at the lavish auditorium in the center of town. Diana had to work that night and Aunt Vi had company from out of town. There was a terrible crash on the highway leading out of Briarton, a car speeding around a curve and veering into the wrong lane. It crashed head on with Aunt Vi's car that Mr. Denny had been driving. When Cindy woke up in the hospital, blinded for the rest of her life, she had blamed Mr. Denny for the accident. He had been seriously injured himself, but had recovered long months later, although he still walked with a slight catch in his back. The driver of the other car had been killed.

Diana gave the old man another comforting pat. "I'll keep praying, Mr. Denny. Prayer can work miracles. In a little more time I know Cindy will learn to forgive and stop blaming you for what happened."

And God, thought Diana. What a trial to befall a new Christian. Her sister had surrendered her heart to the Lord only a few weeks before the accident. Then almost at once she'd had to exercise faith muscles she'd scarcely had time to start building. *Was it any wonder she had withdrawn into herself, hurt, confused, doubting?*

And now the only time she seemed to be anything like her old self was in Chris Jarrett's presence.

• • •

Saturday morning after Diana left for work, Cindy put a favorite gospel record on the stereo and began giving the apartment a thorough cleaning. After polishing the furniture and vacuuming the carpets, she put fresh linens on the beds and scrubbed the bathroom with vigorous care. In the kitchen she cleaned up the breakfast dishes and wiped all the surfaces till they gleamed brightly in her blind eyes.

When her housecleaning was finished it was time for lunch and Cindy settled down at the kitchen table with a glass of cold milk and a plate of crackers spread with crunchy peanut butter. Glad that her weekly chore was complete, she turned her thoughts toward more pleasant lines. At least they would be pleasant if *he* would come to visit again. It had been such fun having Chris Jarrett come for cake and ice cream. And when he had called to talk to Diana last week and she had been at work, he talked so kindly to her. He hadn't been in a hurry and he had been genuinely interested in what she told him about school and church activities, even though she had not much to tell him. Who wanted to participate in something when you couldn't see how? Oh, sure, she didn't *have* to see to do so many things. But everybody else she knew could see. (All those she'd known before the accident.) It wasn't fair that she couldn't see, too.

Cindy left the kitchen table and went into the living room. Chris Jarrett's tender baritone was pouring from the stereo in velvety softness:

Soon we'll come to the end of life's journey
And perhaps we'll never meet any more,
Till we gather in heaven's bright city
Far away on that beautiful shore.

O they say we shall meet by the river,
Where no storm-clouds ever darken the sky,
And they say we'll be happy in heaven
In the wonderful sweet by and by.

If we never meet again this side of heaven
As we struggle thru this world and its strife,
There's another meeting place somewhere in heaven
By the side of the river of life;
Where the charming roses bloom forever,
And where separations come no more,
If we never meet again this side of heaven
I will meet you on that beautiful shore.

Would Chris and she never meet again, wondered Cindy. *It had been two weeks and he hadn't come for another visit. Sure, he had tried to call Diana, but she really didn't like him all that much, and if she didn't encourage his interest he would soon stop calling. Wouldn't he?*

At the stereo Cindy took the stack of records from the turntable and began putting them back into their protective jackets. *If only Diana hadn't been so hurt by Glen,* she thought as she worked. *Maybe she would like Chris a little more. But Chris wasn't like Glen. Why couldn't Diana see that? Because she didn't want to.*

With an empty afternoon stretching before her, Cindy wandered around the apartment feeling lost and forlorn. She could go over to Beth's or Corey's to pass the time. It was just a short walk to either of their homes in the subdivision behind Aunt Vi's apartments. But she didn't really want to be with her friends today. They did their best to make her life much the same as it was before, but her life would never be the same again, and sometimes she got tired of everybody's efforts. Even Diana's and Aunt Vi's. Why did they encourage her to get involved in school and church activities? Didn't they know none of that mattered anymore? When all she could see was grayness and shadows, did anything really matter anymore? She smiled. One thing did. *He* did.

And she had tonight to look forward to. The Jarretts would be among the quartets singing at the Old-Time Gospel Sing at the auditorium. *But would she get a chance to talk to Chris at intermission?* There were always so many people around. *If only...*

Cindy brightened suddenly. Hadn't Chris said when she talked to him on the telephone last week that his quartet would be rehearsing at the auditorium on Saturday afternoons before the concert? He might be down there right now!

Chapter Six _____

In the bathroom Cindy splashed water on her face and dried it quickly with a small towel. If she went down to the auditorium this afternoon she would surely get a chance to talk to Chris after the quartet's rehearsal. Then she could invite him for another visit. He wanted to come to see Diana anyway. He had talked a lot about her on the telephone.

In the bedroom Cindy took her hairbrush from the dresser and gave her glossy, reddish-brown curls several vigorous strokes. Then she pulled off her soiled jeans and shirt and slipped on a clean pair of jeans and a comfortable knit top. She buckled on leather sandals and stood up to smooth her clothes over her tiny figure. Satisfied that she looked present-able, she reached into the closet again and emerged with her cane.

Downstairs she eased out the front door and crossed the col-umned porch to the walkway. At the edge of the walk she paused, taking in the activities of the neighborhood. Cars hur-ried along Franklin Highway just beyond the shopping center, the whine of their motors bringing a constant murmur to her ears. Along Briar Court a gentle breeze ruffled the tree branches and the sun beat down warmly upon her head.

Somewhere she heard the distant sound of a barking dog. Moving her cane from side to side in a low arc, she went along the sidewalk, passing children playing on lawns nearby. She heard the sounds of a ball bouncing to and fro on someone's walkway. Everyone called friendly greetings. She returned them eagerly.

At the corner of Langford Road, Cindy squared off at the intersection and came up to a cautious stop at the curb. She listened for auditory clues. There was no traffic to be heard along the road. But in a minute she picked up the gentle scuff of tennis shoes on the sidewalk.

"Hi, Cindy, where you goin'?"

"Hi, Jamie" she answered, recognizing the voice of a boy who lived in her aunt's other apartment building. "I'm going over to the auditorium."

"What for? Nothin' goin' on till tonight."

"I know," she said. "Do you see any cars in the parking lot, or a bus maybe?"

Jamie glanced across the street. "No bus. Just a couple cars," said the blond-haired little boy. "I gotta' go now, Cindy. I gotta' go to the post office for my mom."

"So long, Jamie," Cindy called as the boy took off up the walk toward the shopping plaza.

Guided by the sound of parallel traffic when it moved along the highway in accord with the signals of the light, Cindy crossed over to the auditorium's parking lot at the Franklin Highway intersection. At the double doors of the brick building she felt for the knob. She gave it a twist and stepped inside. She stood beyond the door and listened. It was quiet in the lobby, but not far away the sound of voices drifted toward her. In the background a piano's keys tinkled in her ears.

Cindy had started forward, toward the sound of the piano when she sensed someone moving in her direction, their footfalls muffled on the thick carpet.

"Hello there, young lady. Can I help you?"

Cindy immediately identified the voice as that of the announcer. "Yes, sir. I was wondering if Mr. Chris Jarrett is here."

"No, ma'am, he isn't here right now."

"Oh," she said, suddenly heartsick, then renewed hope grew in her voice. "Are you expecting him today?"

The man was thoughtful for a moment. "Yes, I believe he did say they'd be here this afternoon to go over some new arrangements for tonight."

"Would it be all right if I waited for him?" Cindy asked, excitement rising in her tone.

"Well, I don't know. We don't usually—"

"Oh, please," Cindy cut in gently. "I won't get in anybody's way or anything."

The man gave Cindy a scrutiny she was unaware of, taking in her neat but casual appearance and her slender, white cane. He was wondering what a blind girl could possibly want with the lead singer of one of the South's most popular gospel quartets.

"Like I was saying, we don't—"

"Is Mr. Art Ross here today?" Cindy cut in again. "He's a good friend of my aunt's, and a friend of mine, too. I know he wouldn't mind if I waited for Chris—for Mr. Jarrett."

"Do you know Chris Jarrett, young lady?"

Cindy beamed proudly. "Yes, sir. He's a friend of mine, too."

"All right," the announcer said, a smile coming through his voice. "Why don't you take a seat inside the auditorium. Your friend will probably be along soon."

He led Cindy through a door across the lobby and left her in a seat on one of the back rows.

In a short while some of the members of The Jarretts Quartet came laughing through the rear door of the auditorium. When all the singers and musicians had arrived, talking and joking around the soft drink machine in the back hall, a man approached them from down the hallway.

"Oh, Chris," he said, walking up to the singer.

He turned. "Yes, Eddie?"

"There's a young lady waiting to see you in the auditorium."

Chris glanced, smiling, at his cousin. "Some fan couldn't wait till tonight," he teased. "She probably wants an autographed picture."

"Of the group," said Billy. "Who'd want to look at your ugly mug all by itself?"

"I don't know what good a picture would do her," Eddie said into their laughter. "She couldn't see it. She's blind as a bat."

Chris looked surprised. "That must be Cindy." He started for the door behind the stage. "Did she say what she wanted?" he asked as he left the group.

Eddie walked with him along the hall. "No, she just asked for you. Said you were a friend of hers."

"I sure am," Chris said, disappearing into the main room of the auditorium.

Cindy could hear him coming at a brisk pace along the center aisle. She liked the sound of his footsteps, even muffled on the carpet they were easy, bouncy, like a joy-filled child's.

Chris made his way past the rows of seats until he came to where Cindy was sitting, smiling now and holding on to her cane.

"Hello, honey. Where'd you come from?"

"I just thought I'd walk down here and see if you were rehearsing," she said, beaming up into his face. "I hope it's all right."

"Sure it's all right. We're getting ready to go over some new arrangements." He studied her quietly for a minute. "Is that the only reason you came down? Is anything wrong?"

"Oh, no, nothing's wrong. Well...I just thought we might not get to see you tonight—at intermission, I mean. There's always so many people."

"If it weren't for the people, I'd be out of a job," he said kindly.

"I'm glad so many people like your music. It's just that...is it okay if I sit here and listen to the rehearsal?"

"That's fine, honey. Why don't you come down front."

Cindy got up and Chris took her arm and led her to a seat near the stage.

It was two hours later before the members of the group left the stage and disappeared into the rear lobby again. Chris jumped down from the platform then and walked up the aisle to Cindy's seat. He sank down next to her.

"How'd you like our new songs?"

"I think they're wonderful. You all really have a special way of singing. You've got the greatest voice in the whole world, Chris."

"Thank you, honey," he said sincerely.

She sat with her blind eyes aimed at him. "You really like singing gospel music, don't you?"

"Yes, ma'am."

"Why?"

"Because I love the Gospel. I love to sing about it."

"When other quartets sing, it's good, you know what I mean? But when your group sings there's something different about it. You all put so much feeling into what you sing, especially you, Chris. I can really tell what you sing comes right out of your heart. Do you make a lot of money singing gospel music?"

Chris chuckled at the girl's expertise at conversational gear-shifting. "We're a long way from being rich, Cindy, but we aren't exactly on the brink of starvation either."

Cindy gave the singer a big smile. "Someone's coming," she said then.

Chris looked up as his cousin came strolling across the stage in their direction. Billy Jarrett was a slim, tall young man with wavy blonde hair and deep brown eyes.

When Billy had joined them, standing in the aisle, Chris introduced him to Cindy. "Did you call Marlene?" he asked the tenor.

Billy nodded. "She's doing fine."

"Billy's wife is expecting a baby," Chris said by way of including Cindy in their conversation. "They just found out the wonderful news, but the way Billy acts you'd think the kid was due any minute."

They laughed and Chris glanced toward the stage as hollow footsteps sounded across the wooden floor. "Will you excuse me a minute, Cindy?" he said. "I have to talk to one of our musicians before he leaves."

"So you're a fan of gospel music," Billy said as Chris strode up the aisle and hopped onto the stage.

"Aunt Vi sorta raised Diana and me on it. Your quartet is our favorite. I bet you're glad to have Chris singing with you."

"Chris is the best I've ever heard," Billy said, taking the seat his cousin had vacated. "I don't know anybody who can touch his range. And he's got an ear for music and a photographic memory that's hard to believe. Did you know he only has to hear a song once or twice and he can remember every note, every word, every chord? It just comes naturally to him. He seldom has to read the music, only if he isn't familiar with a song. But I think he knows practically every gospel song that's ever been written."

"He's more wonderful than I thought!" Cindy said.

"It's a gift," Billy replied, "A gift God gave Chris. He never takes any credit himself for his talent, as incredible as it is. He's worked very hard to get where he is, though."

When Chris returned he addressed Cindy from the aisle. "Are you about ready to go home, little lady?" He flicked a glance at his watch. "It's after five o'clock."

Cindy rose at once. "I'd better hurry. Diana will be home and she doesn't know where I am. I didn't tell Aunt Vi I was coming down here."

"I'll walk with you," Chris said.

Cindy smiled shyly. *He wants to go home with me to see Diana.* This notion made her heart swell with happiness.

Cindy and Chris entered the apartment to find Diana busy in the kitchen.

"Is that you, Cindy?" she called from the range. "Been over to Corey's or Beth's?"

When Cindy didn't answer, her sister turned from her cooking. She was stunned when she looked up and saw Chris in the doorway. *And did she feel something akin to sweet pleasure, too? No! Absolutely not!*

Cindy hurried into the kitchen, spilling out the afternoon's events before Diana had a chance to ask questions or speak to their company. "Is that pork chops you're cooking?" she said at the finish. "They sure smell good." Cindy turned back to Chris who was still standing just inside the door. "You'll stay and eat with us, won't you, Chris? Diana always makes gravy and spoon biscuits with pork chops. She makes the best spoon biscuits you ever ate. Better than Aunt Vi's."

His brilliant gaze locked with Diana's and to her great consternation she discovered herself smiling at him.

"Maybe Diana wasn't planning on a third for supper," he said.

"Oh, there's plenty," Cindy assured him. "Diana always cooks plenty. You never know who might drop in. Sometimes Mr—" She stopped. Then she made her way quickly over to the hallway. "Come on, Chris," she said over her shoulder, "We gotta wash our hands before we eat."

The singer gazed uncertainly at Diana. "Will I be intruding?"

The smile that had dissolved in her face came back. "You're welcome to stay."

When they were seated at the table, Diana asked their guest to offer thanks for their food before she began passing the platter of meat and bowls of mashed potatoes and black-eyed peas. After the biscuits and gravy came around, Cindy spoke up.

"Chris, how long have you been singing?"

"All my life. They tell me I could carry a tune before I was two years old." He paused, smiling. "I used to stutter pretty bad when I was little. My daddy used to stop me from talking and start me to singing. That took care of the stuttering every time, until I finally outgrew it."

"Does your daddy sing?" asked Cindy. "He used to sing with your group, didn't he?"

"He used to be the bass singer in the group. He had a severe heart attack two years ago. He had to retire after that." A sudden sadness filled Chris' beautiful eyes. "I sure miss him not going with us anymore."

"I guess it was hard for him, too, at first," Diana put in.

"Harder for him than for me, I think. But he seems content now to stay on the farm with Mom. But he can't do a lot and I hate that he's so limited now."

"Does your mom sing, too?" Cindy wanted to know.

"Yes, but she doesn't think she's very good."

"I guess not. Compared to you, who would?" Chris laughed as Cindy went on. "You come from a real musical family, don't you? Do you have any brothers and sisters?"

"No. Just a whole lot of aunts, uncles, and cousins. The guy who plays bass guitar with the group is one of my cousins. The guy on lead guitar and our drummer are brothers. More cousins. We met our piano player through them, and our rhythm guitar player is a relative of his."

"What does your bus look like?" Cindy asked.

"It's a big Greyhound. We've had it painted real nice with our name on it. It's fixed up to sleep eighteen people. Sometimes it seems like our second home."

"Diana said you're about thirty, Chris. Are you really that old?"

Across the table Chris' blue eyes twinkled warmly at Cindy's sister. "Yes, I am. But thirty isn't so old. I've got a lifetime ahead of me."

"If you're that old, Chris, why aren't you married?"

"Cindy! I don't know what's come over you tonight," Diana said, while glancing apologetically at their guest.

But Chris only hooted with laughter. Then he said, his velvet drawl marked with good humor, "No, Cindy, I'm not married. I was miraculously rescued from that near state one time and one close call is enough for me."

"Cindy, if you're through grilling our company," Diana said, rising from her chair, "I'll get dessert."

"None for me, please," Chris said, putting up his hands in a gesture of refusal. "If I eat anymore I won't be able to sing a note tonight."

When they had finished the meal, Cindy got up at once and began clearing away the dishes.

"You wash and I'll dry," Chris said, coming to his feet and reaching for a pile of dishes she had stacked.

Across the table Diana rose, too. "You don't have to do that," she said.

"I know." He strode to the sink with the plates. When he came back, he said, "You've probably been working all day. Why don't you go relax for awhile. Cindy and I will take care of this."

She was about to offer a protest, but he cut her off. "Go on. This kitchen isn't big enough for three dishwashers."

Reluctantly, Diana left them, but instead of going into the living room to relax she went into her bedroom to dress for his concert.

Cindy filled the sink with hot sudsy water and began scouring each dish. She had given Chris a towel for drying and as he took a plate carefully from the rack in front of him, he said, "How can you tell when they're clean?"

"I tell by feeling."

Soon Chris had a stack of plates dried and ready to put away. He reached up to open a door by his head.

"They don't go there," Cindy said, "over here on this other side."

When he had put away the plates he watched Cindy. In a minute he said, "You missed a spot."

"Oh, thanks. That happens sometimes."

Chris walked around Cindy with a second stack of dishes. "They don't go over there," she said. "They go back where you were."

"Why didn't you tell me before I walked over here?" he teased. "What if I drop them?"

"They'll break if you do that," she said with a giggle. He stared at her. "I thought you'd know where they go from the last time."

"How could I know that?"

"By looking. I can't see, but I know where they go. Can't you look at what's already in the cabinet and see they don't go there?"

Chris paused, grinning at her. "I don't do this sort of thing for a living, you know."

Cindy giggled again.

"The only reason you know where they go is that you probably arranged the cabinets in the first place."

Diana did and I didn't think she made them very complicated."

Chris laughed then. "Oh, getting smart, are we? Okay, Miss Smartie, what about those dishes over there?"

"Where?"

"To your left and up a little."

Cindy reached out and eased her hand along the counter till she felt the handle of a cup. "I thought I had them all."

"You aren't as smart as you think you are," Chris retorted.

"But I have an excuse. Do you?"

He was about to fire back a reply when a burst of laughter reached them from the living room. Chris turned to see Diana, looking lovely in a gray and white striped skirt and a lacy white blouse, watching them with an expression of patient humor in her eyes. She had twisted her long hair into a knot on top of her head and it gave her a look of cool sophistication that he couldn't resist. He left Cindy at the sink and went around the table.

"You look good enough to take out," he said impulsively.

"Thank you, but I already have plans tonight." To his disheartened look, she added. "I'm taking my sister to hear this crazy gospel singer who likes to dry dishes."

"Oh," he said with a joyous laugh. He couldn't really take her out tonight, but he had been hoping she was going to his concert. "Don't let that get around about the dishes. It might not be good for his reputation."

Diana joined his laughter and in a minute, he said, "Maybe I could take you out one night next week. I'm free Thursday night."

"I'm sorry, Chris," she replied, "I have to work Thursday night."

Diana knew if she were totally honest with herself that she could like Chris Jarrett more than a little bit. He was so good for Cindy, but she liked him for himself, too. He had so many fine qualities. He was intelligent, kind, humorous, talented, and most importantly he was a Christian. But all this was what she feared. She didn't want to like him. *What if he only seemed to be all these things and then...*

She was still too afraid to trust any man yet. Perhaps she never would.

"Another time then," Chris said, and tried not to sound disappointed.

• • •

At the Briar Ridge Auditorium, Chris hastened through the back door and was met by two members of his group.

"Where have you been?" his uncle wanted to know. "We open the show tonight."

Chris glanced at his watch. "Take it easy, Uncle Don," he said good-naturedly.

"Chris boy, you've got to do something about the way you lose track of time."

"I've never missed a show yet, have I?"

Uncle Don shook his head. "You must be courting again, boy. You always forget the time when you're courting."

"I'm not courting...exactly," Chris said.

"Well, where *have* you been?" Billy said, speaking up for the first time. "When you left here with Cindy, I didn't expect you back."

Chris laughed. Then he said, "You wouldn't believe me if I told you."

"Come on, try me," Billy said.

Chris gazed mischievously at his cousin.

"Well, what were you doing?" Billy insisted.

"Dishes," Chris announced at last, then disappeared down the hall toward their dressing room.

Billy stared after him and Uncle Don shook his head again. "He's been doing some little gal's dishes and he doesn't think that's courting?"

Chapter Seven _____

"Just a Little Talk With Jesus," was pouring from the stereo in the living room. Cindy sat at the kitchen table absorbed in a pile of homework. Her concentration broke when she heard footsteps in the hallway outside. She bolted from the chair and hastened to the door. The buzzer had barely sounded when she called out, "Is that you, Chris?"

"Yes."

She opened the door wide, greeting him with a jubilant smile. It had been more than a week since the gospel sing, and though Chris had called Diana twice since then (she'd been at work one night and had gone to a movie with some girl friends the other time), Cindy was a little surprised at his visit. Surprised and *so* pleased.

"Come on in," she said, closing the door behind him and moving toward the stereo.

"Don't turn it off," Chris said. " 'The Eastern Gate' is one of my favorite old gospel songs."

"Mine too," she said, but at the end of "I'll Fly Away" she turned the volume down. "We can talk better," she told him. "That's what Diana always says."

"How did you know I was at the door just now?" he asked from where he had taken a seat on the couch. He had discarded his jacket and dropped it on the loveseat by the door.

"I can tell by your footsteps," she said, collapsing into the wing chair beside the stereo. "By the way you walk." She giggled. "But I'd know you anywhere. Because of all that after-shave lotion you wear."

"My trademark, huh? The *Brut*."

"Well. . .I don't think you'd have to be blind to smell that."

It was Chris' turn to laugh. And then he said, "So you can tell who everybody is by the way they walk?"

"Everybody walks differently. Like Aunt Vi—her steps are slow and heavy, except when she's really in a hurry. Diana moves light and quiet most of the time."

"What else can you tell about people?"

"I can tell a person's height by the direction of their voice when they're standing. Mrs. Jennings, in the apartment next door, is real short and she's not fat at all. Her steps are light and quick like Diana's."

"Does it matter now what people look like?"

Cindy was surprised by his question. For a minute she looked blank. "I guess not, not anymore. No matter what people are like on the outside, we all feel the same things inside."

"You understand people real well for a little lady your age," Chris said.

"I have to be able to tell about people on the inside now, because I can't see what's on the outside."

"Perception it's called," he said, glancing briefly around.

Sensing his movement, Cindy said, "Diana ain't home tonight. She's working."

"Doesn't she have any regular nights off?"

"Her nights off rotate every two weeks."

Chris checked his watch. "What time does she get off?"

"Nine. But it's a little after before she gets out of the store."

"Do you mind if I wait for her?"

Cindy's face lit with delight. "I'd be glad for you to stay. I was just doing some dumb ol' homework before you came."

Chris laughed at her. "How do you do your schoolwork?"

"I use the Braille writer on the table over there." She got up. "Here, I'll show you." She came back carrying a grey metal device that looked and functioned much like a miniature typewriter. She sat down beside Chris and when she had shown him how to work the six large keys, three on each side of the space bar, she said, "I'm not real good at using it yet. It'll take me about another year."

Chris examined the sheet of paper in the Braille writer. "Explain Braille to me."

"Well, everything is done in a combination of six dots—a code of small raised dots based on a 'cell,' a combination of the six dots, three dots high and two dots wide. Altogether, sixty-three different patterns can be formed with the dots to make letters, punctuation, and numbers to produce the equivalent of the print code. You can write music with Braille, too."

"Speaking of music, yours has gone off."

"Do you want me to put on some more?"

"Only if you want to."

She smiled shyly at him. "I'd rather talk to you."

"All right. What do you want to talk about?"

She placed the Braille writer on the coffee table. "Where did you learn to sing, Chris?"

"I suppose I inherited my ability from my family. My daddy and Uncle Don taught me everything they know. I used to sing in the choirs at church and the chorus at school. When I was fifteen I started taking voice lessons, right after my voice changed. I took lessons for about six years."

"You're lucky, Chris, you've got more talent than most. You can sing such pretty soft notes and low notes and you can sing the high ones, too. I bet you could be rich and really famous if you sang different kinds of songs and went out on your own."

"I'm rich in what really matters, honey. Anyway, I like what I'm doing. I've had some offers to go out on my own, but I hear it gets mighty lonely up on top of the mountain all by yourself."

"I wouldn't let you get lonely," she said. "I'd come up on the mountain and see you."

He reached out and rumpled her hair. "I'll just bet you would," he laughed.

"Where will you be singing next?"

"We did a concert over in Sherwood last night. We go to Woodvale tomorrow."

"How do you know where you'll be singing next?"

"That's part of my job as manager of the group, to keep up with all that. We're booked up as far as next spring right now. People call and ask us to give a concert on a certain day or night and we fit it into our schedule. Mom takes care of the bookings when we're out of town."

"I used to sing in the choir at church. I sang in the school chorus, too."

"Why did you quit?"

Cindy shrugged. "I changed schools."

"Don't they have a chorus at the school for the blind?"

"Yeah."

"What happened to the church choir?"

"Nothing." Unaware of his thoughtful scrutiny, Cindy said, "I guess I just lost interest."

"In music?"

"Well..."

"In what then?"

"In...just...about everything."

"Everything? Life? God?"

"I said *everything*."

The girl couldn't know Chris realized the battle she was fighting in her gray solitude.

"Are you a Christian, Cindy?"

"Yes, I guess so."

"Either you are or you aren't."

"I gave my life to Jesus and three weeks later, what'd I get?"

Chris knew it was trial enough to face life's struggles as a growing Christian. But Cindy was a brand-new babe, and to take on such a staggering crisis without time for spiritual growth would be overwhelming, yet God would help her if she would call on Him instead of blaming Him as she was obviously doing.

"Chris, what would you do if you lost your voice like I lost my sight?"

"I love singing for the Lord," he began after a hesitation.

"I'm not sure what I'd do if I had to quit. But God gave me my voice and that makes it His to use. I wondered a lot about this after my daddy's heart attack. Some day it could be me, I thought. But—" He stopped, drawing in a sigh of frustration. "Cindy, your blindness is the result of an accident, a part of life. And we have to deal with what comes our way, but we don't have to deal with it without God."

"What's that got to do with anything?"

"Sometimes we're responsible for things that happen to us. Sometimes someone else is responsible. And Satan is at the root of so much. Then some things just happen—at random, you might say. We don't always know why or even who or what causes them. Life holds so many mysteries. But I do know this: If we are His, He will use us no matter what comes our way— if we are willing to be used."

"You wouldn't blame God if you lost your voice, or had to stop singing like your daddy did?" Cindy said, cutting right through his words to the heart of the matter.

"I wouldn't. No. I see God as the Giver of all good things, not a taker. But certainly He must allow good and bad if He's God and if we are not all just puppets."

Cindy thought about this for awhile. Finally she said, "But if He loves me, then how..."

"How can he let you be blind?" Chris finished for her.

When she nodded mutely, seeming almost on the verge of tears, he leaned over and placed a comforting arm about her slender shoulders. "He loves you, Cindy, no matter how it might seem to you right now. He loves you enough to die for you, enough to suffer to pay for your sins because so great a thing as sin requires so great a price as death. He loves you enough to come back again and take you to heaven with Him. Maybe, somehow, through not seeing, you'll actually be able to see this more clearly."

"What do you mean?"

"You can see your need of Him better, in a way that people who have sight can't. Through the loss of your vision He can help you to depend on Him more, which is what we all should be doing. Testing makes us strong. Hebrews 11 says out of weakness we're made strong.

"As great as your loss is, it's nothing compared to what you've already gained in Him."

"But why did this have to happen to me? Nothing is worse than being blind."

"Helen Keller said the greatest tragedy is not to be blind, but to have eyes and not see."

"How can you have eyes and not see?"

"Plenty of people seem to do it. They have the blessing of sight and do not see what *really* matters."

"Everybody says my faith is being tested. Are tests supposed to last a lifetime?"

"I don't know. They seem to in some situations. You trusted God when you had sight. Why not trust Him now? He's the same God."

"I'm not the same Cindy."

"What about inside?"

"What would you think of me, Chris, if I told you I hated God?"

"I wouldn't think any less of you, if that's what you mean. But what I think of you really doesn't matter. It's what you think of yourself that counts."

Cindy was quiet for another period of time, considering the wisdom of his words. "But why did He have to let me be in that accident?"

"How could He have prevented it without taking forceful control of our lives? In 2 Corinthians, chapter two, Paul says, God is made perfect in our weakness, and His grace is sufficient for us if we love and trust Him. He can still use you now."

"How?" It was almost a plea.

"You'll have to let Him guide you in that. He will if you open up to Him again."

They heard someone at the door just then and Chris looked up to see Diana coming inside. He rose and went to greet the look of surprise on her face.

"Hi, I've been waiting for you," he said with his sweet, intimate smile.

She returned his smile and put down her purse on the loveseat. "That's very nice of you."

"Here, let me help you," he said as she began undoing her coat.

When he had helped her out of the dark blue wool and laid it next to her purse, Diana said, "Would you like a cup of coffee?"

"Thanks," he replied, following her into the kitchen.

Cindy joined them, cleaning her homework swiftly from the table. "I'd better be getting to bed."

Diana, quick to pick up on her sister's obvious gesture to leave her alone with Chris said, "You'd better finish your homework first."

"I'm almost done." With an armload of books and papers shoved haphazardly in her leather case, Cindy beamed radiantly across the table at them. "Well, good night, you two." She moved to her sister's side and kissed her cheek. In a whisper she said, "Doesn't Chris smell divine?"

Diana was still laughing when Cindy said good night to Chris and disappeared into her bedroom closing the door behind her. "There goes your biggest fan."

"She's a great kid."

An even greater kid when her favorite singer was around, thought Diana, *and a scheming one.* She gazed into Chris' face with worried eyes. What was she going to do about this man? Cindy was crazy about him and he was the only person who could cheer her. But Diana didn't want to get involved with him. And she wouldn't, not even for Cindy. It would be wrong to cultivate his friendship only because he gave Cindy so much happiness. It would be using him to do that. Yet, if he didn't quit calling and coming around, she might get to caring for him as much as Cindy had. She had promised herself she would never lay her feelings open that way again. She must keep that promise. No matter what.

Chapter Eight _____

The following Saturday night Cindy, Beth, and Corey went with Aunt Vi to the Old-Time Gospel Sing. At intermission, when the little group trooped out to the lobby for some refreshment, it was with a thrill of pleasure that Cindy felt a gentle hand come up and take her arm and a familiar golden drawl sounding in her ears.

"Hello there, little lady," Chris said.

Proudly, Cindy introduced her adored friend to her aunt and to Beth and Corey.

"Aren't you selling records tonight?" Cindy asked him.

"I just took a break to get a Coke. We have to go back on in a few minutes and open the second half of the show." He paused, looking around. "Isn't Diana here tonight?"

"Oh, she couldn't come," Cindy said. "She was writing a letter to our parents and she had lots of homework to do. Then she was gonna work on the roughs for some ads for Marshall's."

"That young man sure was disappointed because Diana didn't come," Aunt Vi said as she watched the singer stride away across the crowded lobby a few minutes later.

"Yeah, I know," said Cindy. "He really likes her, but she doesn't like him much at all."

•   •   •

Monday night Diana didn't have to work. She had caught up on her homework that afternoon when she got in from

63

classes, and now Cindy and she were sorting their soiled linens and clothes to take downstairs to the laundry unit in the basement.

As they worked quietly side by side in Diana's bedroom, she was half expecting the telephone to ring. It had been almost a week since Chris' last visit. He usually managed to try to get in touch with her in that length of time. Evidently he was working tonight. How ironic it seemed to her all of a sudden that they never had the same nights or weekends free. But wasn't she glad? This coincidence saved her the distasteful task of having to refuse to go out with him. It was so easy to always have a legitimate excuse. She had one every time he asked, like right before he left at the end of his last visit. And the occasion before that when Cindy invited him to stay for supper. But she really had no excuse for not attending the concert Saturday night. Oh, she had wanted to write to her mom and dad, and she always had assignments from her art classes to do, but she could've just as easily finished all that yesterday afternoon.

Admit it, Diana, she told herself. *You stayed away from the concert on purpose. Who are you more afraid of, Christopher Jarrett or yourself?*

Cindy picked up a cotton blouse and began folding it with extreme care. This strange gesture jolted Diana out of her uneasy thoughts. "What are you doing?"

"What? Oh, the blouse," She shrugged. "I don't know. Just thinking, I guess." She tossed the blouse into the laundry basket at her side. "Diana, why don't you like Chris?"

What did this mean when both of them were sitting here thinking of the singer? wondered Diana.

"I do like him, I've told you that."

"Then why don't you go out with him?"

"I've never been off when he's asked me."

"Sooner or later you'll both be off the same night. Then what?"

Yes, then what? "I don't know."

"It's Glen, isn't it?" Cindy asked, adding a soiled pair of socks to a basket of undergarments.

Diana paused with an arm full of bath towels. "I don't want to talk about Glen." She crammed the towels into an already overflowing basket.

"Why do you want to make Chris pay for what Glen did?" Diana stared open-mouthed at her sister. "Don't be silly."

"That's what you're doing."

"It isn't like that at all."

"How is it then?"

"Look, honey," she began, and her voice took on the placating tone she adopted when speaking of something unpleasant to her sister. "I'm just not ready to...to get involved with anyone yet."

"Going out on a date with Chris doesn't mean you have to 'get involved,' as you put it."

"That's how it starts."

"If you were ready to get involved, would you choose Chris?" Diana smiled a smile her sister could not see. "I might."

"When will you be ready?"

"I don't know." Never actually, she thought. The way Glen had hurt her, how could she ever trust a man again?

Glen had seemed so...so good, so considerate, so spiritual. *How did a girl tell? She wasn't old enough to have a world of experience, but didn't basic instincts count for something?* Glen had appeared to be all she thought. He had given every indication of having the same set of beliefs and values and interests she had. He had especially seemed to care as much for her as she did for him. But when a man could fool you so easily, it wasn't any wonder a girl was left wary, left wondering about her own good judgment. *Had she been blind to his faults, more blind than Cindy was now?*

Glen hadn't shown very many flaws in their two years of dating. She knew he had a mild temper and enjoyed having things go his way (who didn't), but they had never had any serious quarrels. Looking back, it seemed she did most of the giving in their relationship, but Glen had never asked anything of her that she hadn't been willing to give, except when he requested they not wait until her parents got furlough and could come to the wedding. On that one point she had been unyielding, and Glen had given in easily enough after a time. *Had that been where it all started?* Or started again would be more accurate. *Had that been when he had...*

Even now, almost two years later, she didn't like to think of what he had done. How he had deceived her. *But wasn't it better to have found out before the wedding? What if she had married Glen, believing, loving, promising? What if he had waited until later to tell her?* She would have been devastated now instead of just cautious. And instead of being nice to Chris, she would have shunned his attention firmly that first night when he had walked them home. As it was she was growing to like him more and more. And that just wouldn't do!

"I hope you don't wait too long to let Chris know you like him," Cindy was saying. "He's bound to give up after a while."

That's exactly what she would do, Diana decided then. If she kept putting Chris off, with real excuses or imaginary ones, he would eventually give up as Cindy said. That way she wouldn't have to speak out finally and maybe hurt his feelings.

If that was what she was going to do, then why did she feel so low all of a sudden? Chris Jarrett's striking features played across the screen of her mind. Because he was really such a grand Christian man. He had gone out of his way to be kind to Cindy and take an interest in her and if there was anything insincere about him he wouldn't take time for that. Would he? Could he be cultivating a relationship with Cindy only to get to her? But he hadn't even known Diana when he sang for Cindy on her birthday. Still, they met him right after the concert and he had been in constant touch with them since.

• • •

"Good night, Frank," Diana called to the assistant manager as he let her out the front door of Marshall's. It was nine-twenty when she had finished counting the money in the cash drawer in her department and turned it in for the night deposit. As she started along the well-lighted parking lot, the dark of night filled the clear sky. There was but a slight moon on this chilly October evening, but an impressive display of stars blanketed the heavens in diamond-like splendor.

A stirring of the wind ruffled her hair as she caught sight of a car signaling out on Langford Road to turn into the parking area. She was nearing the entrance now and the lights of the car shone brilliantly in her face when it came into the lot. She gave a start when the car eased to a stop as she drew up alongside. The man inside rolled down the window and smiled. "May I give you a lift?"

For a moment Diana kept walking. Then she realized that she knew the man's voice. She turned and went back. When she looked into the car window, vivid blue eyes stared back. "Chris, I didn't recognize you at first."

He smiled again and to Diana's supreme consternation she felt a deep wave of joy pour through her. "Get in. I'll take you home."

"Thank you, but I'm used to walking. It isn't far."

"I know. But I don't think you should be out alone."

"In Briar Ridge?"

"All right. So Briar Ridge has always been as safe as the White House. I'm just looking for an excuse to get you in my car."

"Oh?" She grinned mischievously. "And then what?"

"You'll have to get in to find out."

"And if I refuse?"

"You're getting cold. Get in."

"In this woolly thing?" she said, glancing down at her blue coat and gray slacks.

"You're not cooperating at all," he laughed.

She hesitated a minute longer before going around behind the car to the other side. Chris leaned over, holding the door open for her, and as she settled comfortably inside she couldn't help noticing how handsome he appeared in brown corduroy slacks and bulky yellow sweater. The clothes did a lot toward emphasizing the hard muscles and wide shoulders of his lean body. He looked fresh and clean, as if he had just stepped out of the shower and he smelled of that familiar shaving lotion he liked to wear so much of. Gazing across the seat at him, she saw that his honey-brown hair was still damp and brushed softly away from his face. His firm lips were shaped in a dazzling white smile and in his blue, blue eyes she saw the same expression of warmth and approval they'd held for her at the auditorium when they met.

"Where to now, angel?" he said.

"I'm not your angel," she said crossly.

Chris only laughed. "Maybe not mine, but you're an angel. You look like one. You talk like one—most of the time—and you've got angel eyes," he said into the green-gold depths of her gaze. "Not that I've had a lot of experience with angels," he added in a minute. "But you remind me of what I think one would be like."

"I suppose I should say thank you," she said, half-smiling.

"You don't have to. Well, where to?"

"You said you were taking me home."

"Yes, but now that I've got you in here, that's the last place I'm taking you. Have you eaten?"

"Yes."

"Since I haven't. Would you go with me to get something to eat?"

"Do I have a choice?" This was delivered in a tone of pleasant good humor.

"If you really don't want to go, I wouldn't insist."

Oh, darn him! He is so sweet!

She smiled. "I'll go. But we won't be too long, will we? Cindy will wonder where I am."

"We'll call her from the restaurant." Chris had turned his car around and pulled back onto Langford Road before he spoke again. "What do you think of Cindy's attitude about her blindness?"

Startled, Diana said, "Has she talked to you about how she feels?"

"A little. She blames God, doesn't she?"

"God and Mr. Denny." She told him the details of Cindy's accident and her refusal to have anything more to do with their aunt's handyman. "She even gave back the beautiful wandering jew he grew for her. She loved that plant. She kept it in her bedroom. She'd give away all our other plants too if I'd let her. Mr. Denny gave them to us."

"She's young," Chris said. "She didn't have time to grow spiritually in her Christian walk before she lost her sight. Not that it wouldn't still be a trauma."

"She's really a good, sweet girl. In some ways she's not growing up as fast as other girls her age. And I'm glad. Even before the accident she didn't like a lot of the music kids play today. And she used to experiment with makeup, but she's never wanted to wear any out. Now I'm wishing she would take an interest in *something." Besides you,* Diana added silently. "The first year would be the hardest the doctor told us. Cindy's been going through a process of grief and shock. Chris, do you think she'll gradually overcome her bitterness about everything?"

"I think most of us have coping abilities we don't know we have till we're called upon to use them. If she will let God work in her life she can turn what happened into a victory. If not...but she seems all right most of the time."

"Oh, but that—"

When she didn't go on, he took his eyes briefly from the road to glance at her. "That's what?"

Should she tell Chris what a difference he had made in Cindy's life? Would that thrust more responsibility at him than he had time to carry? The kind of person he seemed to be would take seriously the girl's admiration, especially considering the extenuating circumstances. On the other hand, if the singer weren't the sincere person he appeared, then nothing she told him would have much effect.

In the end her concern for Cindy's welfare won out in Diana's battle with her conscience.

"It's just that Cindy looks up to you so much. I'm sure you can understand that. You probably have to deal with that all the time. But with Cindy it's more, I'm afraid."

"What do you mean?"

"Oh, it's not that she has a romantic kind of crush on you.

Not now. But she cares deeply for you. Maybe like an older brother." *Or future brother-in-law,* thought Diana. "The truth is, Chris, she cares so deeply for you that . . . that you're the only one she comes out of her depression for."

This remark sent another brief glance in her direction. "Really?" His tone was grave, concerned.

"Before her birthday party, Aunt Vi and I had about given up on helping her accept her blindness. She . . . well, she wouldn't do anything anymore."

"She told me she'd lost interest in everything, except music."

"Your music."

"I'm glad you told me all this," Chris said.

"I didn't intend to really. I hope you don't feel—"

"I don't," he broke in gently. "I doubt if I have as much influence with her as you think. But if I can do anything to help her, of course I want to."

At the apartment Cindy met them at the door, a jubilant expression on her face. "What are you all doing back so early?"

"Early?" Diana retorted. "Do you know it's almost midnight?"

"That's not late for old people like you."

"Was that a direct hit at *old* Chris?" the singer said grabbing Cindy in an affectionate hug and ruffling her hair.

"You are pretty far gone," she teased.

To which remark, Chris walked slowly about imitating an elderly man's gait and moaning for Cindy to get him a rocking chair to rest in.

A few minutes later Chris was preparing to leave, but before he said good night Cindy spoke up and invited him to go to church with Diana and her the coming Sunday morning.

"If you don't have to sing somewhere," she finished.

"No, we're not singing anywhere Sunday."

"Oh, boy!" Cindy cried, "Then you'll come?"

"Cindy, maybe Chris would like to go to his own church Sunday," Diana put in before Chris could reply. "He probably doesn't get to do that very often."

"Oh sure," Cindy said, and neither Chris nor Diana missed

the note of disappointment in her voice.

But all this little scene did for Chris was create a crossroad of decision. Diana could tell he would like nothing better than to accompany them to church next Sunday, but her expression, she knew, told him she would survive the day quite well without him. As for Cindy, she would be sad and hurt if he didn't go. After what Diana had told him this evening, she realized it was important to him to do what little he could for Cindy, even at the risk of antagonizing her sister.

Diana was unaware, however, that Chris didn't intend giving up on her yet. Every moment he could grab in her presence told him that she was all he had ever dreamed a woman could be. She had intellect, courage, warmth, and gentleness. Above all else, she shared his faith in the Lord. He would be a fool to deny that she was what he wanted.

"Cindy, I'd be delighted to attend church with you next Sunday," he said. Then to Diana: "If your sister doesn't object— too much."

"Diana would love to have you go," Cindy said blithely. "Wouldn't you, Diana?"

She bit down on a flare of anger. After all, if Chris *could* help Cindy . . .

She smiled up into the singer's handsome face, a smile that didn't touch her eyes, he noticed. "I think that would be fine."

Chris' footsteps had scarcely died away on the stairs when Diana turned on her sister, "Cindy, I know you didn't mean to be so obvious, but—"

"Don't be mad, please!"

"You mean that was really deliberate?"

"Yes."

"You're meddling, girl!"

"I'm sorry."

"You're not."

"Well, you won't encourage Chris."

"I went out with him tonight, didn't I?"

"That was nothing. He just picked you up from work."

"Cindy, I'm not going to start dating Chris Jarrett no matter what you do."

"See. I told you."

"No. I told you. Right from the beginning."

"But—"

"Look, honey, I'm sorry. I know how much you like him. I know you want him to keep coming around."

"He won't come just to see me."

"How do you know? He's your friend now, too."

"It's you he really likes. I'm just a kid."

"I don't think he'll stop being your friend even if I don't go out with him."

And somehow Diana felt as if this were really true. Somehow she sensed that Chris was sincere in his concern for Cindy, and that while he might not come as often if she weren't dating him, still she didn't think he would forget her sister all together. There was a tenderness about him, a compassion, a genuine Christian spirit that touched her.

Oh, why did he have to be such a great guy! And why couldn't she treat him indifferently the way she wanted to from the start? How had he managed to find a chink in the protective wall she'd thrown up about herself after Glen's deception?

Maybe she couldn't answer the questions she kept tossing at herself, but she could build her wall a little firmer, thicker, higher. She could oust Chris Jarrett from her life before he did anymore of his charming, treacherous damage. And she could start the very next Sunday.

Chapter Nine_____

Sunday morning Cindy dressed in a red plaid skirt, navy sweater and matching jacket. She stood in her bedroom brushing her long hair till it felt almost silken beneath her sensitive fingers. When she heard Diana go into the living room she put down her brush and started for the door.

Cindy knew what her sister was wearing to church this morning. She had asked her before they showered. She would have on a fitted suit in a light camel color. A slender skirt went with this suit and Diana always wore a lace bib blouse with a bronze string tie at the neck. With her chestnut hair brushed out and curled gently on the ends she was a knockout in this suit.

Cindy giggled as she left her room. That's what Diana would do all right. She would knock Chris Jarrett's gorgeous eyes right out of their sockets!

In the living room Diana was pacing back and forth on the carpet. Diana never paced. Cindy knew why she was doing it now and immediately felt guilty. Chris would be here any minute and Diana truly didn't want him to come. She was sticking her nose in where she shouldn't, Cindy decided. But Chris was such a wonderful person. Why did she keep fighting it? Any woman who couldn't see what Chris Jarrett was had problems with her sense of reasoning. Oh, Cindy knew she was strongly prejudiced in his favor until they had met. Then she was prepared to be treated as nearly everyone else treated her, as The Poor

Little Blind Girl. But Chris made her feel... worthwhile... equal... accepted.

If only Diana would learn to accept him.

Chris arrived in a gray pin-stipped suit in the latest wool blend, and with him he brought an atmosphere of cheer and warmth that stayed with them as they walked the block and a half to the red brick church.

"What's the world look like this morning?" Cindy asked the singer as he strolled along between the two girls.

"It's a beautiful day, honey. The sun is shining and all the trees are changing bright colors. Like God taking a giant paint-brush and stroking the whole world with His special, vivid splendor."

"That's a pretty good way to describe fall," Cindy said. "Do you suppose He likes to look down in winter when everything is white? White's for purity. I think He'd like everything to be pure again."

Following the Bible study time and worship service, Chris escorted the girls back to their apartment. "How would you two ravishing young ladies like to go out to dinner this after-noon," he suggested lightly as they approached the front of the apartment house.

"We'd love it!" Cindy cried, bubbling over at once with her youthful enthusiasm.

But Chris was observing Diana. Her intuition told her that he was pleased with how lovely she looked this morning, and she realized he could also tell she was much less enamored with his idea than her sister. For a minute she wondered why he kept wasting his time. Even if he obviously wanted to be with her more and more, she didn't want to be around him *at all. She didn't!*

Diana saw a look of puzzlement come over Chris' face then. Was he wondering why she offered him so little encouragement? Maybe he thought she cared for someone else. But, knowing Cindy, she probably told him that her sister didn't have a boyfriend. So *what* must Chris think? That he just didn't have any appeal for her? Well, whatever was bothering him, from his expression, Diana knew he hadn't figured it out on his own. Perhaps he would soon be asking her questions she didn't want to answer.

"It's very nice of you, Chris, to offer to take us out," Diana said. "But I'm sorry I can't go."

"Don't tell me you have to work this afternoon?" He smiled affably. "Just my luck."

"No, as a matter-of-fact I don't. I have some... some other things I need to do."

"Hey, no problem. I understand." But did he?

When Chris turned to Cindy she looked totally crestfallen. For an instant he ventured another glance at Diana. She was staring at her sister with a look of incredible hurt in her lovely angel eyes.

"It'll just be the two of us then," he told the young girl.

"You mean you still want *me* to go?"

Diana couldn't keep from smiling as Chris gave her another quick glimpse. At least he would never be able to accuse her of trying to use him to cheer her sister. Of course she wasn't that kind of person, but as little interest as she had shown in him maybe that's what he thought.

"I'm sorry Diana couldn't go with us," Cindy said later as she rode along in the car beside Chris.

"You wouldn't let me go out and eat all by myself, would you?"

"I don't believe you have to eat by yourself."

"Mom and Dad would probably let me have something at home."

"You're teasing me."

"I wouldn't do that."

"Don't you have a girl friend, Chris? Or something?"

He glanced over at her and laughed. "Or what?"

"Oh, you know what I mean."

"No, I don't have a girl friend."

"But you're so good-looking and so talented and so nice and—"

"Hey, wait a minute. I'm taking you out to dinner. You

don't have to heap on the flattery."

She laughed at him. "Why don't you have a girl friend?"

"Maybe because I'm so ornery."

"You're teasing me again." When Chris made no comment, Cindy said. "I guess I ask too many questions."

"Do you like barbecued ribs?" Chris asked in a minute.

"I love them!"

"I know a place where we can get some that are so good you won't believe it."

• • •

Tuesday evening Cindy was alone in the apartment putting away the supper dishes and singing softly to herself. Chris stepped inside the open doorway and stood listening. In a minute he said, "You sing very well, young lady."

Cindy whirled around, a wet dish slipping precariously in the towel she held. It went crashing to the tiled floor. Chris closed the door and rushed across the room. "Honey, I didn't mean to scare you half to death."

"Well, you did," she said. "How did you get in anyway?"

"The door was ajar."

Cindy looked uncertain. "Corey must have forgotten to close it when she left. She left right after Diana did."

A frown creased his brow. "Diana's not home?"

"She went shopping with one of her girl friends," Cindy said, "but she won't be gone too long. Why don't you wait for her? Go and sit down. I'll clean up this mess."

"Let me help you."

"I can do it."

"It's my fault. You might cut yourself. I'll clean it up."

"I'm not helpless."

"I know that, but you have a few limits."

"Only a few," said Cindy stubbornly.

"If you'll just tell me where the broom is?"

A short time later Chris joined Cindy on the couch. When he reached into the back pocket of his slacks she spoke up. "What are you doing?"

There was a moment of silence. Then he said, "I was getting out my handkerchief to wipe the blood off my finger."

Cindy giggled. "Seems like you have a few limits, too," she said smugly.

"Don't we all?"

"I'm sorry."

"About what?"

"I'm sorry you cut your finger. Will you let me have your handkerchief?"

"Whatever for?" he asked in an incredulous tone.

"So I can take it to church and show everyone Chris Jarrett's blood."

Laughing uproariously, he reached out and rumpled her hair.

"A lot of people recognized you Sunday," she said. "The girls in my class couldn't believe it when I told them we were friends. Will you really let me have your handkerchief?"

"I will not."

Cindy sat beside him, giving an excellent imitation of a proper pout. He smiled a smile she couldn't see and said, "I meant what I said awhile ago. You have a trainable voice, Cindy. Your sense of rhythm is good and you have a fine clearness of tone."

"Do I really?" she said, brightening again. "I've been told I can sing. The choir director at church and the music teacher at school both said so."

"I think you could be more than good in time. You have real potential." Into the silence that followed, Chris said, "But you have to use your voice under a competent instructor if you're going to develop it."

"Like in choir and chorus?"

"Yes."

"You think I should get back in the choir at church?"

"And chorus at school." After another silence, Chris said. "Let's sing some right now. My guitar's in the car. I'll go down and get it."

"You play the guitar?"

"Not enough that you can really tell it."

"Yeah, I'll bet. What else can you play?"

"I fool around on the piano a little."

"Like Liberace probably," Cindy said amazed. "Do you play anything else?"

"I suppose I can beat out a pretty fair sound on a set of drums."

"What else?" she said, awestruck now.

"Nothing much. I like to mess with a banjo sometimes. And an accordion. I like to play the organ, too."

"Where did you learn to *play* all those instruments?"

"My daddy can play about anything. Uncle Don plays, too. I learned from them, but I picked a lot of it up just fooling around I guess."

"Billy said you had a special ear for music, but I didn't know you could sing and play both."

"I have a lot of fun with it," he said, rising. "I'll be right back."

Chris returned shortly carrying a shiny brown-gold flattop guitar. He let Cindy examine it before he slung its wide strap over his shoulder. "What'll we sing first?"

"You sing. I'll listen."

"I want to hear what you can do."

"You first."

"What do you want to hear?"

"I don't care."

Suddenly Chris gave a riotous shout of laughter and began strumming away outrageously on the guitar. In a sharp country twang he lifted his voice in a silly rhyming song. At the conclusion he doubled over in laughter at his own nonsense.

Cindy couldn't help laughing with him. Then she said, "Would you like to sing songs like that all the time?"

As quickly as his festive mood came on, Chris banished all trace of it. "No, honey. I only want to sing about Jesus. Because if I didn't proclaim Him every time I open my mouth I wouldn't be doing the job He's given me to do. I wouldn't be living up to my name either."

"What do you mean?"

"Christopher means 'Christ-bearer.' It's more than an honor

and a responsibility for me to bear Christ to the world. I was named to do it."

"Your mother told you that?"

"Yes. I grew up singing for Jesus. She dedicated my life and my voice to Him when I was very young."

"Oh, Chris, that's the most beautiful thing I've ever heard. Sing something about Jesus now."

"You sing with me. How about 'His Hand In Mine'?"

"I love that one. You do such a good job on the low parts."

Chris and she joined their voices then:

You may ask me how I know my Lord is real,
You may doubt the things I say and doubt the way I feel.
But I know He's real to-day, He'll always be,
I can feel HIS HAND IN MINE, and that's enough for
    me.

Chris handled the deep notes of the chorus by himself:

I will never walk alone, He holds my hand;
He will guide each step I take, and if I fall,
I know He'll understand.
'Til the day he tells me why He loves me so,
I can feel HIS HAND IN MINE, That's all I need to
    know.

"Beautiful job, Chris."

"Thank you."

Next they blended their voices on the old gospel tune "Farther Along." At the finish, Chris said, "Let's sing some more real old ones."

They went through "A Beautiful Life," "On The Jericho Road," "I'll Meet You In The Morning," and "Kneel At The Cross" before coming to a stop.

"You sing one by yourself now," Cindy said, a little out of breath.

Chris laughed and for a time sat strumming a few chords quietly on his guitar. Then: "I think this is one of the most beautiful songs ever written. It's about fifteen years old. The melody is pretty and the words say exactly what should be in the heart of a Christian.''

Cindy leaned back against the cushions of the couch as the velvet richness of Chris' baritone poured over her:

When I think of how He came so far from Glory....
came and dwelt among the lowly such as I....
to suffer shame and such disgrace;
on Mt. Calvary take my place
then I ask myself a question....Who am I?....

Who am I that a king would bleed and die for?....
who am I that He would pray 'Not my will thine,'
    Lord?....
the answer I may never know; why He ever loved me so;
that to an old rugged cross He'd go, for who am I?....

When I'm reminded of His words, 'I'll leave thee
    never....
just be true I'll give to you a life forever'....
I wonder what I could have done to deserve God's only
    Son;
fight my battles 'til they're won....who am I?....

Who am I that a king would bleed and die for?....
who am I that He would pray 'Not my will thine,'
    Lord?....
the answer I may never know; why He ever loved me so;
that to an old rugged cross He'd go, for who am I?....

It was a long time after Chris finished the song before Cindy spoke. "I've never heard anything so...so...utterly beautiful."

"It's a wonderful song."

"I didn't mean just the song." Her blind eyes reached toward his face. "*Nobody* can sing like you do, Chris. Nobody in the whole world. You know something, if you'd been born a bird they'd have called you a golden-throated warbler. Is your voice insured?"

Chris broke into laughter again. "Honey, you sure are good for my ego."

"Sing something else, Chris, please!"

"You have to sing with me."

"I'll only spoil it."

"Come on now."

"Okay, but first tell me the difference between a gospel song and a hymn. We call them hymns in church, but at your concerts you call them gospel songs."

"We sing a lot of both. A hymn is an anthem, a praise *to* God. A gospel song tells of a relationship *with* God or Jesus. It expresses our testimony to God and it proclaims the teachings of the gospel."

"But all gospel songs aren't Southern quartet gospel music?"

"No. There are all kinds, contemporary, country. Actually, old-time quartet gospel music denotes a style. The difference is in the rhythm. It's an outgrowth of the old Negro spirituals of years and years ago, plus rhythm and blues. The rock 'n roll music of the fifties sprang from this."

"Let's sing something else now," she said.

They were nearly through a robust version of "Reach Out To Jesus" when the front door flew open and Diana burst into the room, her hair flying and her eyes blazing. She closed the door before saying heatedly, "What's going on up here? I can hear you two all the way out front!" She tossed her purse and a paper bag on the loveseat as Chris stood up and took off his guitar.

"I'm sorry. I guess we got a little carried away."

Cindy had risen beside him. She addressed her sister in a small, tight voice. "Were we really that loud?"

"You were!" Diana said, trying hard not to look at Chris anymore. He was so perfidiously disarming standing there in gray slacks and sweater that emphasized the lean hard lines of his broad shoulders and long body. And what his unbelievably blue eyes did to her, she didn't even try to fathom.

Chris held onto his guitar like some errant schoolboy caught putting a tack in the teacher's chair. It was all Diana could do to keep from laughing at him. When he came around the coffee table and approached her, she made herself ignore him and went on talking to her sister.

"Cindy, you know how the McIntoshes are, complaining over every little thing."

"But they live downstairs in the back apartment. You don't think they heard us?"

"If I could hear you out front..."

Cindy looked contrite, and Chris, turning and seeing her expression, truly felt sorry that he had gotten her into trouble. "It wasn't Cindy's fault," he began, but Diana swept his words aside impatiently.

"I think you'd better go."

The muscles in Chris' jaw throbbed and his teeth clenched tightly together as he struggled to control his mounting anger. "Not until you promise not to say anymore to Cindy. The—

"I don't need you to tell me how to talk to my sister," she broke in coldly.

"The noise was my fault," he went on calmly, but it took effort. "I'm trying to apologize."

The sound had been anything but noise, thought Diana. Their duet was beautiful, as any duet would be with Chris Jarrett as half the team, but she couldn't tell him that. Not when she had a ready-made chance to make him so angry he would never come back. She hated to do that because of Cindy. But no matter how fine a friend he became to her sister, no matter how he cheered her, ultimately she had to face her handicap on her own. If she didn't, his kind attention wouldn't have accomplished a thing.

It came to Diana all of a sudden that it had taken her a long time to realize this. But she had finally and she would cling to the notion because she had to protect her own emotions in regard to the singer. One look at him tonight and she knew if he didn't soon quit coming around she wouldn't be able to hold out against his charm or sincerity much longer. In the face of his gentle but persistent onslaught, her wall of outrageous indignation was crumbling fast!

"I accept your apology," Diana said with all the indifference she could manage. "Now will you please go?"

He stared at her a minute longer, resisting an urge to either give her a good shaking or take her boldly in his arms. Which of the two he wanted to do most he wasn't sure. He did neither but instead turned and said good night to Cindy. To Diana he said, smiling slowly, deliberately, "Good night, angel." Then with his guitar in hand he stepped out into the hall and was gone.

Chapter Ten

Diana had closed and locked the door behind him and was gathering her purse and package from the loveseat before Cindy spoke. "I'm sorry we got so loud, but you shouldn't have talked to Chris like that."

At the tearful sound in her sister's voice Diana looked up anxiously.

"He'll never come back now," Cindy said on the brink of a sob.

Dear Lord, help me! Diana silently cried. *What have I got us into? I'm trying to fight this man with every ounce of strength and Cindy's crying for him like a baby!*

She went to the girl's side and took her in her arms. "Cindy, honey, don't cry. He'll come back." *I hope,* her own heart echoed.

"No, he won't," Cindy sobbed. "Anyway, you really don't want him to. Do you?"

"No, but maybe that won't stop him," she said impulsively and immediately wished she hadn't.

Cindy lifted her head. "What do you mean?"

"Nothing. Just remember he's your friend, too, and he'll come back to see you."

She sniffed. "No, he won't."

"You wait and see."

"Why did you get so mad? That's not like you."

"I've never come home and heard you entertaining the whole

neighborhood before." I wonder what Mr. Denny across the hall thought, Diana had been about to add but decided against it.

Cindy smiled sweetly. "Chris is so much fun. Did you know he can play all kinds of musical instruments? And you know what he said?"

She told her sister what the singer had said about the potential of her singing voice.

"I thought you had something pretty special," Diana said, and seeing that Cindy was over her brief crying spell, picked up her things from the loveseat and started for the bedroom. Cindy followed.

"Chris says I ought to get back into the youth choir and chorus at school too."

Oh, bless the man! thought Diana. *Maybe with his help Cindy really would be all right.*

"You don't want to disappoint him," she said, dropping the contents of the bag on her bed and placing her purse on the dresser. She took off her coat, that she noticed for the first time she was still wearing, and hung it in the closet.

"No, I don't want to do that," Cindy said, sinking down on the edge of the bed. She smiled again. "Why did Chris call you an 'angel'?"

Diana grinned in spite of herself. "I don't know."

"It's his pet name for you, isn't it?"

"No!" she said, coming back to the bed.

"Oh, Diana, he must really like you. I bet he thinks you're beautiful like an angel." She giggled. "But you sure acted like a devil tonight."

"I wasn't that bad," Diana said, reaching for a bottle of nail polish.

"It's not like you to lose your temper. Why'd you do it?"

"I told you."

"Were you trying to make Chris mad?" When her sister didn't reply at once, Cindy went on. "That's it, isn't it? You wanted to make him mad. Why? So he really won't come back? Why don't you want him to come back?"

"The answer to that, my inquisitive, intuitive little sister, I don't want to hear. But I guess it's useless to think you won't tell me."

"You don't want him to come back 'cause he's trouble for you. He's trouble for you down in that place called your heart."

How right Cindy was. And trouble of the romantic-heart kind was just what she didn't want or need. Even if she did like Chris, she didn't trust him. She didn't want to go out with him. Dating him could lead to....

She knew what it could lead to and she wasn't about to put herself in that position again. If a man ever hoped to win her heart a second time, he would have to be so special, so far above reproach, so sincere, so spiritual. And so far she had met no one who even came close to all those qualifications. No one except... Chris Jarrett.

* * *

Cindy and Beth walked home from prayer meeting the following evening with Aunt Vi. When they arrived at the apartment house, she invited the girls into her apartment to try some of her homemade cookies. They made themselves at home on her comfortable couch and she served them cold glasses of milk and fresh oatmeal cookies.

Beth chatted away in her usual friendly manner, but Cindy was quiet most of the time. When Beth left for her house in the subdivision, Cindy lingered on the couch. She had something on her mind, Aunt Vi realized, and wondered if she should encourage her niece to unload her burden. It was so difficult to guess what Cindy was thinking these days. Replacing her recent, constant state of depression, she often had days of joy and peace. And while Diana had mentioned the effect Chris Jarrett was having on Cindy, her explanation had hardly been necessary. The radiance in Cindy's face when she talked about the singer, the laughter in her voice, said it all. How pleased her aunt was that someone had at last been able to cheer the desolate girl.

The kindly aunt wondered what could be troubling her niece

tonight. Could Cindy be concerned about something at school or church? It didn't seem likely. For all her renewed spirit and interest in life, that interest seemed to center on only one area. Or more accurately, on only one person. One Christopher Jarrett.

"Aunt Vi," Cindy said, breaking in on the older woman's thoughts. "If you liked somebody, liked them a whole lot, and they were...well...rude to you, would you stop liking them?"

Aunt Vi's thin eyebrows shot up. What was this child contemplating? Could it be...

She had not shown any concern for Mr. Denny since the accident. She had even been rude to him since then, if in her own mind she had reason. Was she finally coming to understand that her rejection of him might have been wrong? These two had experienced such a special fondness for each other that Aunt Vi sometimes wondered if Cindy didn't miss their friendship as much as the handyman did. Perhaps she was missing it now and was wanting to rekindle the spark of their relationship.

"I don't think I would stop liking them, Cindy," Aunt Vi said carefully. "But I might try to understand why they'd been rude, and maybe talk to them about it."

The girl was out with it then, telling her aunt what had taken place the night before. "Do you think he'll ever come back? Do you, Aunt Vi?"

So it was Chris Jarrett after all!

To the anxiety on her niece's face, the aunt said, "Diana told me about your little concert. I'm sorry I was out and missed it."

"You aren't angry about us making so much noise?"

"No, dear. But I wouldn't want such loud singing to become a habit."

"You don't have to worry about that. I don't think Chris will ever come back."

"I should think that depends."

"On what?" Cindy said, a ray of hope sparking her tone.

"On whether he really wants to come back."

"He really likes Diana. But she doesn't like him much. She *says*."

"Oh? You don't believe what she says?"

"I think she likes him more than she lets on."

"Wouldn't it be wonderful if Diana was ready to open her heart to a young man again? And Chris Jarrett seems like such a fine person. But she has been so hurt before. Of course, that was nearly two years ago now. Time enough for the wound to heal."

"If she would let it."

•   •   •

Sunday morning Cindy sat beside her sister in the pew. Aunt Vi sat on Diana's other side, and Cindy, near the aisle, had left room on the seat for Beth and Corey. The service was just beginning and the girl was wondering where her friends were when she felt someone slip in quietly beside her in the wooden pew. This person didn't say anything to her, so she assumed it was someone she didn't know.

The music director started the opening hymn and as everyone stood up Cindy heard Diana reach automatically for a hymn book. Then her sister gasped and let out a quick rush of air. Cindy was about to ask her what was wrong when all around them the congregation began the words to "Amazing Grace." In the next instant Cindy realized what was wrong with Diana. She stood riveted to the spot, her hands resting on the back of the pew in front of her. Music welled in her ears from every direction, but her ears picked up only the golden baritone of the man standing beside her. Then, as if on cue, the familiar fresh scent of his after-shave lotion drifted toward her. She put out her hand and touched his arm. He closed his fingers around hers and she gave him a smile so radiant it pulled at his heart-strings and left them all in a tangle.

After the service Chris was greeted by members who remembered him from his previous visit and by fans who knew him from his records and concerts. When finally he was able to leave the churchyard it was a subdued little group that waited for him on the front walk. The singer greeted them with his usual warmth and charm, smiling and talking animatedly with

Aunt Vi and giving Cindy an affectionate hug.

"I didn't think you'd ever come back to see us," she whispered in his ear.

"You don't have much faith in me, little one," he said softly.

"I do now!" Cindy retorted.

Chris was hooting with laughter when he glanced up from Cindy's shining face and caught Diana's eyes. She kept her expression unreadable, but she could have kicked herself for the tingle of pleasure she felt at Chris' lingering gaze. His look said he found her especially attractive today. She had on a navy suit with a white blouse and red string tie, and her long hair cascaded over her shoulders in lovely soft curls. Considering Chris' own dark suit that so enhanced his tanned good looks, Diana wondered if he thought, as she did, that they looked the well-matched couple.

With a casual arm around Cindy, Chris addressed her sister, "What plans do you girls have for this afternoon?"

Some friends joined Aunt Vi then and they left for an afternoon together at the Briar Ridge Community Center working on Thanksgiving baskets for needy families.

"I have to work this afternoon," Diana said as soon as her aunt and the other ladies had gone.

Chris managed to cover his disappointment. "Do you have time for a hamburger before you go to work? I could drop you off afterward."

"All right. That would be nice," Diana replied after only the briefest hesitation. How could she refuse such kindness, especially after the way she had treated him?

In the parking lot Cindy climbed happily into the back seat of Chris' cream-colored Celica and he opened the door to the passenger side for Diana to get in. She paused, standing with the door open between them and gazing up solemnly into his face.

"I think I owe you an apology," she said quietly. "I really didn't mean to be so...rude the other night."

"You don't have to apologize. It's forgotten."

"No. I am sorry. You've been so nice to Cindy. I—"

"Is that the only reason you want to apologize?"

Diana was uneasy all of a sudden. Finally, instead of giving him an answer, she tore her gaze from his and moved to get in the car. He put a restraining hand on her arm. "Is it?"

"No...oh...I don't know."

"When is your next night off?" he said. "If the group's not singing that night, will you go out with me?"

Diana focused her gaze on the pavement beneath their feet. She couldn't look at him, if she did she knew what her answer would be. Already her hesitation had probably given him encouragement.

"No."

Before she realized what was happening, Chris had taken her chin in his hand, forcing her to look up at him. "Why not?" When she made no response, he said, "What is it, Diana? I'm not too stupid or ugly, am I?"

She couldn't help laughing a little. "Of course not."

"Then why won't you go out with me? Is there someone else?"

"No!" she flared, freeing herself from his hold. "I just don't want to go out with you."

I don't. I don't. I don't.

Chris dropped Diana off at Marshall's. As he left the parking lot and turned onto Langford Road, he glanced over at Cindy seated beside him now. "Would you like to go over to Billy and Marlene's with me?"

"Oh, that's all right. You can just take me home."

Chris' keen ear didn't miss the slight note of dejection in her voice. "I want you to go with me," he said in his drawl that was so soft and gentle.

"Why?"

"Why do you think? Because we're friends."

"Are we really? Even if..."

He laughed. "Even if Diana never goes out with me."

"You've been so nice to me already. I don't know how I can ever be a real friend to you. I wish I could do something nice for you."

Chris stared at her for an instant before he slipped a comforting arm around her shoulders. If she could have seen the expression on his face she would have known what he felt. Since she couldn't, the tenderness and understanding was there in his voice. "You do something nice for me every time you smile, honey."

"That's not much for a friend to do."

"It's more than you think. Anyway, real friends don't always have to do things for each other. Being a real friend sometimes means just being there."

"I'll always be there for you, Chris, if you want me to. I promise."

Taking his eyes quickly from the road, he leaned over and brushed the top of her head with a kiss.

"Do you have a boyfriend, Cindy?" he asked a short time later.

"No."

It was such a solemn, pathetic little response that Chris wondered if he had said the wrong thing. "But you're so good-looking and so talented and so nice."

"Hey, you're teasing me!"

"I wouldn't do that."

Into the silence that followed, Cindy finally said, "I'll never have a boyfriend, Chris, because I'm blind."

"What's that got to do with it? I've got big feet and crooked fingers, but I don't think I'm too obnoxious."

"Do you really have crooked fingers?" She faced him. "Let me feel them."

Chris held up his right hand and Cindy began to trace the shapes of his long fingers. "Your hands are big," she said in a minute.

"I've got big feet, too. And a big mouth."

She laughed. And then, "Hey, your little finger is sorta crooked. It doesn't go straight out like the others. It curves inward at the end. Let me see your other hand."

Dutifully, Chris took hold of the steering wheel with the hand Cindy had been examining and offered her his other one.

"This little finger is crooked too," she said before long. "Chris with the crooked fingers."

"Nobody's perfect," he said, placing both hands back on the steering wheel. "Does this mean we can't be friends anymore?"

"Oh, you! Quit teasing me!"

"I wouldn't do a thing like that."

"What's that ring you wear on your right hand?"

"It's my college ring. From the Christian college over in Belle City."

"Diana wants me to go to college."

"Of course you'll go."

"So I can get a good job to support myself. If I can. It's for sure no man will want to help take care of me."

Chris gave his passenger a silent scrutiny she wasn't aware of, trying to imagine what it was like to be blind. She had told him once that it was like being in gray shadows all the time, but not a total void or complete lack of vision, still, being without sight had to be traumatic, especially at first.

"I don't think that's true, honey."

"Aunt Vi doesn't either. She says Craig Jarvis is a good example."

"Who's Craig Jarvis?"

"He's a new boy at church. He's fifteen. He seems pretty mature. Aunt Vi says he stares at me all the time."

"Your beauty probably has him spellbound."

"Do you think what I look like could sorta make up for being blind?"

"It could, but I hope you know neither of those things are what really matters."

"You're not blind, Chris, you don't have any idea what really matters."

"I know it's tough, honey, very tough for you right now, but it's not the end of the world."

"Did you grow up on a farm?" Cindy asked, proving once again how adept she was at changing the subject. When he answered in the affirmative, she said, "Tell me about it?"

"It was hard work, but it was a lot of fun too. Everybody had to do his share."

"Did you have lots of animals?"

"And a big garden and hay fields. There's a creek that winds through the farm. It runs along beside the house and there's lots of shade trees, some big oaks and sycamores."

"It sounds nice."

"It's the only home I've ever known. It feels good now to go back there when we've been away on tour. It's beautiful and peaceful out there. I love the life. I think you'd really like it too. Maybe sometime soon I can take you out there. You and Diana."

Cindy grinned. "You'd like that wouldn't you? If Diana could go?"

"Yes."

"Maybe next Sunday. Diana won't be working then."

"We're singing in Charleston next Sunday." Chris guided the car into a sharp right turn. "We're almost to Billy and Marlene's," he said.

Soon Chris parked his car in a paved driveway and Billy met them at the door of a small brick bungalow. A pretty, fair-haired young woman in slacks and full smock joined them in the living room.

After Chris introduced the girls, Cindy and Marlene chatted pleasantly for a few minutes, until Marlene said, "I was putting some things away in the nursery before you came, Cindy. Why don't you come and help me?"

The men watched them disappear down the hall to a room at the end.

"I thought it was her sister you were so interested in," Billy said to his cousin.

"I don't think she's too interested in me."

"You mean she's still resisting all your charms?"

Chris laughed. "She's doing real well so far."

Billy slapped his cousin affectionately across the shoulder. "You can't win them all, Chris."

"I know. But I'm not giving up on this one yet."

Chapter Eleven _____

It was the Monday evening after Thanksgiving. "Known Only to Him" flowed softly from the stereo in Chris Jarrett's rich, Southern baritone. In the kitchen Cindy was sitting at the table lost in a homework assignment when she heard lively footsteps mounting the stairs in the hallway. She rose and hurried to the door just as the buzzer sounded.

"Is that you Chris?" she called.

"You mean you didn't recognize me?"

Laughing, she flung open the door. "Hey, I smell pizza!"

"And Cokes," he said, coming inside and glancing around.

"That's my favorite. How'd you know?"

"I took a wild guess. You look like the pizza and Coke type to me." He placed a large flat box and a paper bag on the table. "Diana's not home?" he said, shrugging out of his jacket and hanging it over one of the wooden chairs.

"She's working," Cindy said on the way to shut off the stereo.

Chris' gaze fell on the fragrant plant decorating the center of the table—the angelwing jasmine, Flower of Romance. It reminded him of Diana. He wasn't having much luck with her, but how often did a man meet an angel? Better not let her get away.

"I tried to call," he told Cindy, "But the line was busy."

"Diana was talking to Nellie. They're best friends."

"Have you had supper?" he asked as he opened the box of pizza.

"Two hours ago. But I can eat pizza anytime!"

"I thought you might be tired of leftover turkey."

"I am. But we had a great Thanksgiving dinner with Aunt Vi. What did you do for Thanksgiving?"

"Ate too much," he said with a laugh. "We had a whole houseful of aunts and uncles and cousins come to dinner."

While Chris took Cokes from the paper bag, Cindy got small plates from the cabinet and brought them to the table. "Do you want a fork to eat your pizza with?"

"A fork will probably keep me from getting so much of it on my clothes."

They both laughed and after Chris offered thanks for the food they sat across from each other talking comfortably.

"What kind of clothes do you wear?" Cindy asked suddenly.

"Ordinary clothes, I guess."

"What are you wearing now?"

"Gray slacks and a velour shirt. It's burgundy."

"What kind of clothes do you wear when your group is singing?"

"Usually suits, or shirts and pants sometimes. We match them up."

They had finished eating and were starting to clean up the table when out in the hall there came a loud thud. Then came another and a dull boom, then one final thud.

Chris was on his feet at once. "What in the world was that?"

"I don't know," Cindy said, following his steps to the door.

In the hallway, doors to several other apartments were thrust open and curious occupants emerged. Quickly, Chris moved to the white wrought iron railing surrounding the staircase hallway. At the bottom of the steps he saw Aunt Vi bending over the shape of a man. Nearby lay an overturned pot. It was broken and dirt had spilled onto the carpet.

In one hasty stride Chris went around the railing and down the stairs. The others in the hallway came after him.

Chris kneeled beside the man who lay stretched out on the carpet. He was large and heavyset with gray hair and a stubble of beard. To Aunt Vi, Chris said, "Can you tell how bad he's hurt?"

"I'm not hurt. I'm all right," the man said, his gray eyes coming open to focus widely on Chris.

"You can't be sure yet," the singer said. "You took quite a fall down the steps."

"I didn't fall all the way," he said slowly. "I was about halfway down when I tripped."

"You just lie quietly," Chris said. "We'll get the emergency medical service. You don't know what injury you might have."

"No, I'm all right," the man insisted. "I think I can get up now."

But when he tried, Chris saw him wince with pain and draw a hand almost inadvertently to his lower back. "I think you'd better lie still, sir. We'll get you some help."

"No! No! I'll be fine. I just tripped."

When the old man seemed determined to get up, the singer said, "Here then, let me help you." He put a strong arm around his back to aid him.

"I don't think you should try to go up to your apartment," Aunt Vi said. "Come into my living room and lie down on the couch."

The old man seemed about to protest, but Chris said. "I'll take you over to the emergency room at the hospital. You really should be checked. If you've hurt your back—"

"No, no, I'll be fine," said the man. "I'll just lie down for a few minutes."

Someone in the crowd that had gathered offered to clean up the broken pot and mess of dirt. After helping the old man into Aunt Vi's apartment and staying a few minutes to be certain he was really all right, Chris went back upstairs.

Cindy sat on the couch with her blind eyes fixed on nothing. As soon as Chris entered the living room he sensed a change in her manner. He had guessed the old man who had fallen down the stairs was Mr. Denny, the man Diana had said Cindy blamed for her blindness.

"I'm a little worried about your friend," the singer said,

taking a place beside her. "He may be more hurt than he realizes."

"He's not my friend!" she spat viciously.

Taken aback, Chris stared wonderingly at her. The pain and bitterness she harbored was worse than he had imagined. "It was Mr. Denny—"

"I heard. I'm not deaf, too."

She was nursing a hurt grown big as a mountain. "Diana told me about the accident," he said.

"Don't *you* start telling me how it wasn't Mr. Denny's fault. I've heard all that a thousand times from Diana and Aunt Vi."

"He *was* driving the car."

Cindy was struck speechless with surprise at the emphasis in Chris's words, then said, "He could've gotten out of the way of that other car. I *know* he could. He didn't really try."

"Do you remember exactly what happened?"

She shrugged. "It was raining very hard. The road was slick. The other car just came right at us, around a curve. The last thing I saw was the glare of the headlights in my face."

"The other car was speeding, Diana said."

"Mr. Denny's getting older. He shouldn't have been driving. He doesn't anymore."

"Why not?"

"Would you, if you'd caused someone to lose their sight because of your driving? He told Aunt Vi he'd never drive again."

"So he blames himself, too?"

"Why shouldn't he?" she said disparagingly. "It was his fault."

"There's no one else to blame. The driver of the other car was killed."

Into the long silence that grew between them, Cindy finally said, "You think it was the other man's fault?"

"From what I know of the accident, he seemed to use bad judgment. Driving so fast on a rainy night when roads are bad and visibility is poor."

"You're just like Diana and Aunt Vi!" Cindy flared. "You

don't think it was Mr. Denny's fault either!"

"Cindy, why are you letting Satan have his way with you?" Chris said calmly.

"What do you mean by that?"

"Satan has reached down in his bag of dirty tricks, and he's using one of those tricks on you."

"I don't understand."

"You haven't been a Christian very long, honey, but you *are* a Christian. And the sooner Satan can render you ineffective the happier he will be."

"What do you mean, 'render me ineffective'?"

"In John 10, verse 29, Jesus said the followers God gives to Him—meaning all those who become saved—no one can take away. In other words, if you are truly saved you can never lose your salvation—but you can become a weak Christian and not serve God well. Or not serve Him at all. That's what Satan works on in a Christian's life. That's all he has to work on."

"He's trying to make me weak?"

"He tries to make every Christian weak. For weapons he can sometimes use the things that happen to us. With you it's the accident and your blindness. If he can keep you bitter about it and hating Mr. Denny, then you won't do any work for God. You can't."

"Satan doesn't make me hate Mr. Denny. I don't need anybody to make me do that."

"True. We all have a naturally sinful nature. But Satan uses our nature—he uses anything he can—to tempt us into not serving and witnessing for Jesus." When Cindy made no more comment, Chris said, "You can't trust Satan, honey. In John, chapter 8, it says there is no truth in him. He's the father of the lie."

"But Mr. Denny caused me to be blind," Cindy said.

"Perhaps he did."

"How can I ever feel the way I used to about him?"

"You and I caused Jesus to be nailed to the cross—our sin did, everyone's sin—but His love for us has never changed. It's unconditional."

"So I'm supposed to forgive Mr. Denny like nothing happened?"

"It's sure easier to be forgiven than it is to forgive, isn't it? I suppose that's because to be forgiving we have to be more like God. Real forgiveness wipes out the hurts and bridges the gaps between people. Of course, forgiveness was God's idea in the first place. It's an essential ingredient of love, which God thought up first, too."

"You talk like I'm just supposed to forgive Mr. Denny for some wrong he did to me. Chris, *he made me blind.*"

"No honey. It was an *accident*. He didn't cause it on purpose." After another silence, Chris said, "Cindy, you know the risk you're taking, don't you?"

"What risk?"

"It's explained in one way in Mark 12, and in another way in Matthew 18. If you have anything against another person, you must forgive them because if you don't neither can God forgive your sin. We aren't free to abuse each other without harmful results. God is the ultimate authority in all relationships."

"Be ye kind one to another," quoted Cindy, "tenderhearted, forgiving one another, even as God for Christ's sake hath forgiven you. That's Ephesians 4:32. We had that Scripture in our Bible class yesterday."

"Do you know the Lord's Prayer, Cindy, the model prayer Jesus gave us to guide our own prayers?"

"Matthew 6, verse 12—'And forgive us our debts, as we forgive our debtors.' "

"We can forgive others because God has forgiven us. Jesus recommended unlimited forgiveness in Matthew 18."

"I can't forgive Mr. Denny, Chris, I just can't. Everything's not all right. It never will be. I'm blind now and he's just fine."

"That's true. But what if he'd lost his sight in the accident too? What if he'd lost his life? Would it restore your sight? What could he do now that would give it back?"

It was a long time before Cindy spoke. When she did her voice was barely above a whisper. "How can I want to forgive him? 'Cause in my heart I really don't.''

"Have you prayed and asked God to help you? Ask Him to help you turn a need into a want.''

When Diana came in from work, Chris and Cindy had abandoned their serious talk and had put some gospel music on the stereo and were talking and laughing animatedly.

The look of surprise on Diana's face when she opened the door and saw Chris vanished rapidly as she dug way down in her resources for the strength to resist his sweet, gentle charm. Was that what it had come to now, she wondered? Was she scraping the bottom of the barrel for some meager aid in withstanding his shattering appeal? Was she weakening at last?

He met the force of her stern gaze with an amiable smile, but before either of them could speak, Cindy said, "Diana, you don't have to get mad at Chris tonight. We ain't making a lot of noise."

This remark made them all laugh, but in a minute Diana took off her coat and started for the kitchen. "Will you have a cup of coffee before you go, Chris?" she said over her shoulder.

He laughed deeply from where he lounged on the couch beside her sister.

"How do you take it?" she called from the range.

Chris got up slowly and crossed the room. Stealthily he went up behind her. "Black," he said into her ear.

She jumped and turned around. His face was only inches from hers. She could smell the pleasing masculine scent of his aftershave lotion. "You scared me," she said, trying to steady the unexpected erratic beating of her heart.

"I'm sorry." He gazed tenderly into her upturned face and Diana longed suddenly to know what he was thinking.

As they had coffee at the table, her uneasiness at his presence must have shown, for he soon got up to leave. If she were really so uncomfortable with him, Diana mused, maybe she should ask him to stay away. But she knew he liked being with her, even for only a few minutes at a time. She was sure he kept coming around because he wanted to learn if she were really all he thought her to be.

"You know something?" Cindy said as the girls got ready for bed that night. They were at the vanity in the bathroom. Diana was cleaning makeup from her face and Cindy was getting ready to brush her teeth. "I think Chris really has a thing going for you."

"Why do you think that?"

"You don't think he keeps coming here to see me, do you?"

"Why not? I told you he was your friend."

"He told me, too." She smiled suddenly. "Did you know he has crooked fingers?"

Diana turned from the mirror to stare curiously at her sister. "How did you discover that? Have you been giving him the once-over?"

"He's so sweet, Diana. I don't know why you don't just fall into his arms."

Diana regarded her sister thoughtfully. "Are you thinking about doing something like that?"

"Oh, I don't feel that way about him. But you do. Don't you?"

Diana went back to creaming her face in the mirror. "No."

"Yes, you do. I think you like him a lot."

"I don't."

"You can't fool me. I can hear it in your voice."

"I don't want to be hurt again, Cindy. That's all."

"Chris ain't like Glen. Can't you see that? He's got the real love of Jesus inside of him. He wouldn't hurt you. You know something, Diana, I'm the one who's blind, but I think you're the one who can't see!"

Chapter Twelve _____

Thursday evening, a week after Thanksgiving Day, Diana was trying to get ready for work. But her head kept throbbing and her whole body felt weak. She had been sneezing off and on since the previous day, and from all the symptoms, she had about decided the flu epidemic in the community had finally overtaken her.

"I don't think you should go to work," Cindy said when Diana came into the living room with her coat over her arm.

The buzzer sounded at the door before Diana could form a reply. When Cindy let Chris in, he took one look at her sister and said, "Where do you think you're going?"

"I don't think I'm going anywhere," she replied and promptly began to weave sideways.

Chris moved quickly and grabbed her by the shoulders. "What is it? The flu?"

She nodded as he draped an arm about her. She leaned against his quiet strength and ran the back of her hand over her forehead. "I'm a little dizzy. And I feel so hot all of a sudden."

Chris took her coat and began leading her over to the couch. "I don't think..." she said, but that was all she managed before slipping from his hold.

He tossed her coat on the chair nearby, bent down, and picked her up, gathering her slender form into the gentle strength of his arms. "You're as weak as a day-old kitten." Over his shoulder he spoke to Cindy. "Which one is Diana's bedroom?"

Although her illness made Diana feel terrible, she wasn't without some sensitivity toward Chris. He'd obviously come by hoping to spend a little time with her or even to ask her out. And she was sick! That was one excuse she hadn't thought of. But would even that deter the indomitable Chris Jarrett? When she was feeling better, Diana decided, she really should compliment the man on his extreme determination.

Friday night when Cindy greeted Chris at the door, he stepped into the living room with a shiver. "It sure is cold out."

"Is it snowing yet?"

"I don't think it's going to now." He looked around. "How's Diana?"

"She's asleep."

He shrugged out of his jacket and layed it across the loveseat.

"She's been asleep all day," Cindy went on.

Chris strode to the couch and lowered his lean, broad-shouldered frame onto the cushions. Cindy took a seat in the chair by the stereo.

"Ain't you singing anywhere tonight?" she asked. "I mean, *aren't* you? Diana's always telling me not to say ain't."

"Not tonight. We do a concert in Huntsville tomorrow. We go on down to Birmingham for a big show Sunday."

"Do you want me to go see if Diana's awake?"

"Not right now. Maybe she'll wake up in a little while."

"Aunt Vi made some chicken broth for her. Maybe she'll wake up and want something to eat pretty soon."

"Cindy, why do you think your sister doesn't like me?" Chris asked in a minute.

Startled, the girl said, "Oh, she likes you, Chris. Really she does."

"Did she tell you that?"

"Well...not exactly. But I know she does."

"Do you know why she won't go out with me?"

"Yeah, but I don't know if I should tell you."

"I don't want you to tell me anything that Diana doesn't want you to."

"I don't know if she wants me to tell or not. Probably not. But I think you deserve to know. Diana's afraid of being hurt again. That's why she won't go out with you. At least I think that's why. She was engaged, but her fiance broke it off all of a sudden. Anyway, Glen went with a girl named Rita before he met Diana. When he broke off with Diana he told her it was because he still loved Rita. He'd been seeing her while he was dating Diana, but she didn't know it."

"Do you think she might not want to go out with me because she still cares for this Glen?"

"No. Diana doesn't love Glen anymore. Not too long after he broke off the engagement—it's been almost two years ago—she said she was really glad. She said she realizes now it would've been a mistake to marry him 'cause he was pretending to be something he wasn't."

"And she's afraid to trust again."

"She told me once she'd never give another man a chance to hurt her like Glen did. So now she won't go out with anybody."

Cindy added that she couldn't understand Diana's thinking. Chris could, however. A broken engagement was difficult to forget, how well he knew.

"How's Mr. Denny?" he asked, changing the subject.

"Cindy didn't answer right away. "Aunt Vi says he's having trouble with his back."

"Have you talked to him?"

"No." It was a feeble reply at best.

"Cindy, why don't you heat up that broth," Chris suggested. "Maybe Diana would like something to eat now."

In the bedroom Chris eased across the floor holding the tray Cindy had prepared. At the side of the bed he stopped, gazing down at Diana laying pale and motionless beneath the blankets. When she opened her eyes, she blinked long lashes and looked up at him. An expression of surprise and pleasure greeted his sweet smile.

In his beautiful gaze Diana detected a barely controlled yearning. She sensed he wanted to reach down and take her in his arms and perhaps touch her lips with soft kisses. What would it be like to be kissed and caressed by Chris Jarrett? Could he wipe away her dark sorrows, all the painful memories? She wasn't sure. But she did know she wasn't ready to accept the tender feelings stirring within him. And what saddened her most was knowing she might never be ready.

"Do you feel up to eating a little bit, angel?"

Nodding and stifling a yawn, she said, "What time is it? Have I been sleeping all day?"

"I think so."

She pulled herself up into a sitting position, smoothing the wrinkles in her flannel gown and trying to straighten her mass of hair. Chris placed the tray across her lap, then reached behind her to arrange the pillow so she would be more comfortable.

He sank down on the edge of the bed and Diana studied his handsome face quietly for a moment, enjoying his kindness toward her. But in the next instant she wished he hadn't seated himself in such close proximity. His nearness proved too dangerous to her topsy-turvy emotions.

"Drink that broth while it's hot," he said in that voice that could convey such softness, such tenderness. "It'll build your strength."

"Strength is sure what I need. I have to get out of this bed and go to work tomorrow."

"If you don't mind my saying so, I don't think you should. You'd better stay in bed another day, maybe two. If you go out too soon before you're completely well you might get sick again."

She picked up the cup in front of her and took a sip of broth, observing him over the edge of the cup. "Is that an order, doctor?"

He laughed before giving her an answer. "Do I have to make it one?"

"You don't seem like the kind who orders people around."

"I can get tough if I have to. Just don't push me too far."

• • •

Sunday afternoon Cindy was in the kitchen baking chocolate chip cookies when the telephone rang. "I'll get it, Diana, she said, going through the living room to the hallway. "Hello."

"Cindy, it's Chris."

"Chris! Hi!"

"I'm calling long distance, honey. How's Diana?"

"Oh, she's feeling a lot better. Aunt Vi's here. She brought up some homemade vegetable soup."

"Did Diana work this weekend?

"No. Do you want to talk to her?"

"No, that's all right. I've only got a minute."

"Where are you?"

"In Birmingham. We're going up to Memphis tonight. From there we go to Jackson. We'll be home in a few days. I'll see you then."

Cindy ran back to the living room. Her sister was seated next to Aunt Vi on the couch. "Diana, you'll never guess who that was! He was calling long distance!"

"It wasn't Christopher Jarrett by any chance?"

"He was calling from Memphis. I mean, Birmingham. They're going to Memphis tonight. He just called to see how you were. Oh, Diana, he must be crazy about you to do that!"

"He seems like such a fine young man," Aunt Vi said, entering the conversation for the first time.

"He sounded lonesome," said Cindy.

"I'm sure he is," Diana observed, "traveling with eight other guys."

"He's lonesome for *you*, Diana. He said he'd come over to see us when he gets back."

And I probably won't be here, thought Diana regretfully. She gave herself a quick mental shake. Had Chris Jarrett finally succeeded in breaking through her protective armor? Had being in his arms the other day really felt as good as she remembered? Strong. Protective. Tender. She had known his embrace would be like that.

Cradling the memory to her breast, she trembled involuntarily. It had been worth getting sick just to be held by that man!

Chapter Thirteen _____

Chris came by Tuesday night. Diana had finished her homework and since she didn't have to work she was leaving to meet her friend Nellie for dinner and a movie.

"I'm sorry, Chris, I really am," she said to his request to take her to dinner. "We're meeting a couple other friends and—"

"I understand. I should've called. But we only got back this morning. We drove all night and I was beat."

He doesn't look beat now, thought Diana. He looked wonderful and if she hadn't already agreed to meet Nellie....

Chris waited until Diana had gone before he asked Cindy if she would like to go with him to get something to eat. "Billy's got some new songs he wants me to look at. We could go over there afterward." He paused warily. "Unless you have plans, too."

"I was going over to Corey's for a little while, but I can do that anytime. I'd much rather be with you."

At Billy and Marlene's house the men occupied themselves in Billy's den while Marlene took Cindy into the nursery and let her feel some of the soft clothes that awaited their baby's birth. Cindy's sensitive fingers absorbed every aspect of the new apparel and she marveled at how tiny the infant's booties were.

Later, while the girls prepared a snack, Chris and Billy withdrew to the paneled basement where the tenor proudly displayed track after track of his beloved electric trains.

"I sure hope that baby is a boy," Chris said as Billy flipped the switch on a small transformer.

"It doesn't make any difference. If it's a girl, we'll make a first-rate engineer out of her, too."

Chris laughed, and Billy pushed a button on the transformer. Instantly the caboose became the leader of the row of cars.

"How are you doing with Cindy's sister?" he said a minute later. "Not too well, I guess, or you'd be bringing her over instead of Cindy."

"She won't go anywhere with me." He told Billy about Diana's broken engagement.

"So she's got the same problem you do," his cousin said.

"But Cindy said she's over it now."

"But the scars remain, don't they?" Billy turned off the transformer. "Chris, I know you're not coming to me for advice, but maybe you should forget the whole thing."

"I'm beginning to think you're right only—I can't seem to stop going over there. When we're not working or rehearsing, I find myself in the car headed for her apartment. There's something about her, you know what I mean? She seems to be everything God intended in giving His gift of woman to man."

Billy nodded. "But after what happened before, nobody could blame you if you never trusted a woman again."

Chris thought back to the painful experience to which Billy referred. In a minute he said, "I'm ready to trust again. But evidently Diana isn't."

Billy examined his cousin's expression. "I think you've got it bad again."

"I finally realized tonight that it isn't doing me any good. You think I can find something else to do with my time?"

• • •

Monday night, two weeks before Christmas, Cindy was getting ready for bed when the buzzer sounded at the door.

She pulled on a robe over her pajamas and went to answer it, wondering who could be coming so late. It was nearly ten o'clock. No one ever came past that time on a school night.

At the door she paused with her hand on the knob. "Who is it?"

"It's Chris, honey."

Her face lit up with delight as she welcomed him into the living room. "I was in the bedroom. I didn't hear anyone coming upstairs."

"I would have come earlier but I got to watching a football game and before I knew it, it was almost nine." Chris took off his coat and they sat down on the couch. "Sometimes I'm not very good about keeping up with the time." After a slight pause, he said, "Is Diana here?"

"No, she had to work late. Christmas hours, you know? She'll be here soon, though." Into the sudden awkward silence, she said, "You like football a lot?"

"It's a good sport. I like rugged sports."

"You play football?"

"Once in a while a bunch of us get together out at the farm and fool around."

"It's got something to do with your shoulders," Cindy said. "Diana said you look like a football quarterback—without shoulder pads."

Laughing, Chris jumped up and went to the loveseat to get the package he had left there beside his coat. "Here, I brought you a present," he said, returning to the couch and placing a neatly wrapped package in her hands.

"It's two whole weeks till Christmas."

"I thought you could get a lot of use out of it by then."

"I don't know what to say, Chris. I wasn't expecting you to...what is it?"

He laughed again. "Why don't you open it?"

In a matter of seconds she had the paper torn off and had lifted the lid. She ran her fingers quickly over the contents of the box. "A Braille Bible!" she cried. She picked up the book and began turning the pages. "Oh, Chris, I love it! I love it! I have some cassettes, but this is wonderful! How can I ever thank you?"

"You can read it."

"Oh, I will! I'll read every word!" she laid the book carefully on the coffee table and turned to face the singer. "Chris, you're just the greatest person in the whole world." She reached out with both hands and touched his face. Then she leaned over and placed a kiss on his cheek. "Thank you with all my heart."

"You're welcome, sweetheart," he said, but already she had gone back to the Bible, her fingers flying deftly over the pages.

"I can't believe how fast you can read," he said shortly.

"I like to read. I've trained my fingers pretty good."

Chris sat watching her with deep pleasure in his blue eyes. He could feel her open affection for him and he enjoyed being a part of her life, maybe helping to fill some of her dark hours. He would miss her company very much.

"Diana, look at this!" Cindy cried when she heard her sister come in the door. "Chris gave me a Braille Bible!"

Diana studied the big leather-bound book Cindy held so lovingly in her hands. "How thoughtful of you, Chris." *More than thoughtful. She knew what such a book cost.* She glanced at him.

He had stood up when she came in. Now he was staring at her with his heart in his eyes. Those incredible eyes. Suddenly Diana felt her knees go limp. If he asked her for a date tonight, she would have a difficult time not shouting out her answer!

"Cindy doesn't have a gift for you yet," she told the singer, "but—"

"There's no gift I want from Cindy," he broke in. "She's already given me everything." Her love. Her trust. Her understanding. He didn't say the words, but he didn't have to. Diana could read it in his face.

They stared at each other across the space of a few feet.

The silence was broken only when Cindy spoke up. "I'm going to my room to read for a little while before I go to sleep." To Chris she said, "Thank you for the wonderful present."

She moved to go, but Chris called her back. He walked over to her and wrapped her slender body in an affectionate embrace. "Why, Chris," she said, when he had let her go, "you act like you're never gonna see me again."

"You know better than that, honey. That was just a...a Merry Christmas hug."

After Cindy had gone to her room, Diana said, "She's really excited about the Bible. That's a good sign, don't you think? Maybe she doesn't hate God after all."

"I don't think she really does. She just thinks she does right now."

Perhaps it is the same with her feelings for Mr. Denny, Diana thought. Hoped.

She started for the kitchen. "I'll make some coffee."

"Not for me. I can't stay."

She paused by the table and turned, gazing up at him in dismay. There was something different in the tone of his voice. In fact, now that she considered it, his whole manner seemed different tonight.

"Before I go I have something to say." Even as he spoke Chris strode to the loveseat and picked up his jacket. "I think it's long past the time to say what's on my mind," he began. "There's no sense going on the way things are. I've been coming here a lot and—don't get me wrong—I like being with Cindy. She's precious. She and I will always be friends. But she's just a little girl. I've been coming here mainly to see you. I think you know that. Maybe I've only been making a fool of myself." He paused, staring at her as he slipped on the coat. "I hope I'm not stepping out of line by saying this, but I'd like to spend some real time with you. I want to get to know you better. But I don't want to bother anybody or make anybody angry—most of all you."

He paused for another minute before he went to the door. With his hand on the knob, he turned. "I suppose what I'm trying to say is this—I've been coming...and calling...and coming...but if Cindy is the only one who wants me around, then I won't be coming around anymore.''

He gazed deeply into her startled eyes for a moment longer. Then he opened the door, stepped out in the hall, and the next sound she heard was his footsteps echoing down the stairs.

Chapter Fourteen _____

For an instant Diana was too stunned by his speech to move.
Then she broke from her state of shock and ran to the door.
"Oh, Chris." But even as the words escaped from her lips she
choked them back. She wouldn't go after him. She couldn't.
Pride reigned too strong. She had made herself a promise never
to let another man make her vulnerable, and here she was about
to go chasing off after Chris Jarrett like a...like a teenage
groupie.

What had gotten into her anyway? Wasn't this what she had
been wanting all along? Well, she was rid of him now. And
it was for the best. She was beginning to like him far too much.
So was Cindy. Now they could go back to their lives before
he had sung his way into their hearts, before he had smiled and
laughed his way into their days, before he had been so kind
to Cindy. Before he had...

And what about Cindy? As soon as she realized he wouldn't
be coming back, she would probably return to her earlier depression and listless attitude. Staring at the closed door where Chris
had stood only moments before, Diana wished this was the only
reason for the feeling of desolation that slowly invaded her soul.

• • •

The musicians began to play and Billy raised his high voice
in a favorite gospel number, "Where Could I Go?"

As the music came to a stop, Chris said, "Good evening,

114

ladies and gentlemen. We are The Jarretts and we sing and play for Jesus." With a dazzling smile he went on, "If we look like we're having fun up here, that's because we are. Being a Christian is more fun than anything else we can think of. If you haven't made that commitment to the Lord, we would encourage you not to put it off any longer."

For more examples of the fun Chris had been talking about, the quartet broke into two fast-paced gospel songs—"Joshua Fit the Battle of Jericho" and "Swing Low Sweet Chariot." Then they slowed the tempo with "In The Garden," "He Knows Just What I Need," and "Take My Hand, Precious Lord," featuring Chris' beautiful, expressive baritone.

Intermission was nearly over and Cindy was still waiting by the refreshment stand when she felt a gentle hand on her arm.

"Cindy, it's Chris."

She smiled up into his face. "I know. I can smell your aftershave."

He laughed and reached out to ruffle her hair affectionately. "Are you waiting for someone?"

"Aunt Vi. We got separated in the crowd."

"Come on, I'll take you to find her."

They were about to start off when two teenage girls approached them from across the lobby. "Excuse me," one of them said. "You're the singer who does the talkin' for The Jarretts."

Chris smiled down at them when they didn't go on. "Yes, ma'am."

"Can we have your autograph? Please?" said the same girl. She glanced at her friend and they snickered self-consciously.

"It will be my pleasure, ladies," he said, taking the piece of paper they held out. One of the girls gave him a pen. He wrote his name for them and gave back the paper and pen. "If you'll hurry over to that table," he said, nodding toward the far end of the lobby, "you can get some of the other guys' autographs, too."

"Thank you, Mr. Jarrett," the first girl said, "but we just want *your* autograph."

Chris laughed softly as both girls turned beet-red and ran off across the lobby.

"It's nice to know such an important person," Cindy teased with a giggle.

"I'm not so important as you call it," Chris shot back. "The people are just real nice. They like our music and they treat us fine."

"Especially you."

Chris looked up to see Aunt Vi approaching. "Here comes your aunt," he said.

"Diana's not with her," Cindy added. "She—"

"Honey, I'm sorry to interrupt," he broke in, "but I've got to get ready to go back onstage. I'll see you later. All right?"

"Yeah. Okay. Bye, Chris." Cindy looked blank as the singer paused and spoke to her aunt before striding off over the carpet. Her statement about Diana was left unfinished.

• • •

Cindy felt her way along the hall with her cane, moving it back and forth in front of her in a low arc. At the bottom of the stairs she paused, listening. Someone was in the entrance hall of the building. Everyone who knew her made it a habit to speak and identify himself when they met, so she was puzzled by the silence.

She hesitated by the steps. Whoever was in the hall was standing nearby. She could hear someone breathing. In her mind she pictured the entrance to Aunt Vi's building, the big white door where you came in and the long, narrow panes of glass on each side. Along the staircase were a variety of potted plants and miniature trees.

"Morning, Cindy."

It was Mr. Denny!

She stood at the foot of the stairs as though she had been planted there and had taken root. From the direction of his voice, he was somewhere near her aunt's doorway. He came toward her slowly, and from the sound of his halting steps on the carpet she could tell he still walked with the catch in his back that he had since the accident. Perhaps he hadn't escaped totally unharmed after all. But he seemed to be moving even more cautiously this morning. His back must still be bothering him from the recent fall he had taken. Diana said he refused to see a doctor about the pain he continued to have.

"I was watering the jew," he told Cindy when he reached her side.

She had wondered once or twice about the beautiful plant he had given her. It was now occupying the corner in the hall by Aunt Vi's door. Well, she had made it clear she didn't want it in her room anymore. It was too much a reminder of the old man and what he had done.

"How's your back, Mr. Denny?"

If the handyman was surprised at Cindy's question he tried not to show it. This was the first time she had spoken to him since the previous August. Since the accident, whenever he approached her to make conversation, she would only turn away as though she hadn't heard.

"It's coming along. I—"

When he didn't go on, she said, "Why haven't you been to the doctor?"

"Oh, it'll be all right. I don't need to see no doctor."

An empty silence spread between them. Finally Cindy moved as if to go. She put out her cane and started toward the front door opposite the stairs.

"Going over to Beth's or Corey's?" Mr. Denny called after her.

She paused in the doorway seeming to ignore his question. After another lengthy silence, she said, "Are you gonna eat Christmas dinner at Aunt Vi's, Mr. Denny?"

When the old man, not sure what kind of reply to make, didn't make any for a minute, Cindy spoke up again. "You always eat dinner at Aunt Vi's with everybody. I think she'd be disappointed if you didn't come this year."

It was a Christmas tradition at the apartment house that Aunt Vi made dinner for her family and anyone in her two buildings who didn't have other friends or family with whom they would spend the day. Aunt Vi's son and his wife and two children were always on hand. And Cindy and Diana came, and their parents when they were home on furlough. Usually at least one tenant would join in the occasion, and Mr. Denny, having no other family, completed the holiday. That was until last year when he had still been recovering from injuries he had suffered in the accident.

Aunt Vi had been giving serious thought to the best way of coping with what could be an uncomfortable day for everyone this year. With Cindy refusing to have anything to do with Mr. Denny, her aunt had been undecided about the dinner arrangements.

And so it was with great pleasure as well as mild shock that she received the news from Mr. Denny that he had been given, in an indirect way, an invitation to spend Christmas day with the family.

Chapter Fifteen _____

"What time is it, Diana?" asked Cindy.

"Six-thirty."

"Ain't you gonna get ready?"

"I'm not going."

The girls were in the living room. They had finished supper and Cindy was on her way to shower and dress for the gospel sing. It was New Year's Eve and the first gospel meeting held at the auditorium since early in the holiday season.

"You don't have to work tonight," Cindy protested. "You don't have any other plans, do you?"

"No. Nellie has a date. And so does..." *So does everyone else,* she thought. *Everyone but her. Oh, well, what was she whining about? A date was the last thing she wanted.*

"Haven't you missed Chris?" Cindy pressed her.

How could she miss someone she had only known for a few months, someone she had only seen for the briefest period of time? But she did miss him. She missed him being here often when she got in from work. She missed his smile, his good humor. And it seemed now whenever Cindy put on one of his gospel albums, the sound of his magnificent voice did crazy things to her. Like causing her heart to put on a good imitation of an acrobat, turning foolish somersaults much of the time.

"I think it's funny he hasn't been over," Cindy went on. "He told me the men in the group take off around Christmas to be with their families. He should have a lot of free time. He hasn't called, has he?"

"No."

"I can't wait to talk to him tonight—if I get to. There'll be so many people at the concert on New Year's Eve. Why aren't you going?"

"I don't want to."

"Why not?" When her sister gave no reply, Cindy was thoughtful and reflective. "Chris didn't seem interested in where you were when I talked to him at the last concert. Is anything wrong? Do you know why he hasn't been over?"

Diana had known it would come to this sooner or later. If Cindy didn't figure it out for herself, then she would have to be told. Diana just hated doing it. Cindy had been like a different person since Chris Jarrett had taken an interest in her. Since meeting him she had been more enthusiastic, more vital. And while Diana couldn't be sure, she suspected that somehow Chris had been responsible for her sister's gesture to Mr. Denny right before Christmas.

"Chris won't be back," Diana said finally, almost reproachfully. But who could she reproach? Only herself.

Cindy froze in the middle of the floor. "Why not?"

"Because. . .well, do you blame him? How often did he come by? How many times did he try to call me? How many times did he ask me to go out?"

"You sound like you're sorry he's quit."

"I am." *I'm miserable*, she vowed silently.

Cindy's face was suddenly all smiles and a glow of radiance. She went over to her sister seated on the couch. "You mean that?"

"Yes."

"Oh, Diana, that's wonderful!"

Diana regarded her sister with a look something like disdainful tolerance. "What are you so happy about?"

"You and Chris."

"There is no 'me and Chris.' I told you, he won't be back."

"Did he tell you that?"

"He sure did."

"Well, come on then. Hurry up."

"Hurry up for what?"

"Get ready to go to the concert to see him. You've got to tell him how you feel."

"I'm not going down there and tell Chris Jarrett how much I like him."

"Why not?"

"Because..."

"How's he gonna know if you don't tell him?" Into the silence that followed her question, Cindy said, "If you won't tell him, I will."

"You will not!"

"I will! And you can't stop me!"

"Cindy—"

"What did Chris say to you the last time he was here?"

"He said you two would always be friends, but if you were the only one who wanted him around here he wouldn't be around anymore."

"Diana, can't you see? It's up to you now. That was an open invitation for you to let him know if you like him."

"But I—"

"He's crazy about you," Cindy said, "and if you let him get away you're just plain crazy." She took her sister by the hands. "Come on," she urged, pulling her from the couch, "we'll be late if we don't hurry."

• • •

At the auditorium Chris' group was already onstage when Diana, beside Cindy and Aunt Vi, slipped into a back row of seats near the center aisle. At the sight of Chris, dressed in a white suit and standing beneath soft lights, singing his heart out for Jesus, her own heart swelled with a secret kind of happiness. She was glad now that she had let Cindy talk her into coming. Seeing Chris again made Diana realize that he truly was a special person. She had been wrong to put him off for so long. She only hoped when she talked to him—if she could get near him in this crowd—that it wasn't too late, that he still felt the same way about her.

At intermission the girls made their way slowly out the aisle to the lobby where Diana searched in vain for Chris. It was impossible to get within even a reasonable distance of the long table where the group put out their records on display. And it became equally as improbable that they would soon be able to approach the refreshment stand either. So Diana had to content herself with standing about halfway between these two places and hoping she might catch Chris if he passed.

It was Art Ross she finally succeeded in picking out of the crowd. When the slightly-built frame of the auditorium's owner came by, Diana put out a hand on his arm to detain him.

He smiled and greeted her warmly, then he turned to Cindy.

"We were looking for Chris Jarrett, Mr. Ross," said Cindy. "Have you seen him?"

Art Ross gave Cindy a smiling scrutiny. "I hear from your aunt that you and that young singer have become quite good friends."

"Oh, we have," Cindy beamed, "but it's Diana who was wanting to see him tonight." She grinned innocently at her sister.

The owner of the auditorium turned his gaze on Diana. She blushed self-consciously under his inquisitve examination.

"Chris Jarrett is a fine young man," he said. "And with talent as remarkable as his, he sure doesn't have to worry about his future." After a slight pause, he said, "You say you're looking for him, Diana? If I'm not mistaken, I saw him a few minutes ago heading backstage toward the dressing room." He smiled and winked. "It's the last one on the left as you go down the hall."

Art Ross left them then and disappeared into the thinning crowd. As Diana turned to Cindy she saw the familiar figure of Craig Jarvis approaching. He was the good-looking, dark-haired boy who had been paying so much attention to Cindy lately. More and more he asked to sit with her during church services and sometimes he walked home with them afterward. He had a pleasant, easy-going personality and seemed to be very well-mannered. Cindy didn't talk much about him, but Diana felt his interest in Cindy was good. With her recent loss of vision and her resulting depression, a boost in her self-confidence was in order, Diana thought.

Craig spoke first to Diana and then touched Cindy on the arm. "Hi, Cindy."

She smiled shyly. "Hi, Craig."

"Why don't you go back inside with Craig?" Diana said to her sister. "The second half of the concert will be starting soon. I'll be along in a few minutes."

Backstage, Diana went quickly along a narrow corridor till she neared the end. She slowed her steps not far from Chris' dressing room and paused to collect her thoughts. What would she say when she finally saw him? How did she begin to explain how sorry she was for treating him so coolly? And would he even be interested now? It had been more than three weeks since he had been to her apartment, time enough for him to forget, especially since they'd had so little time together to get to know each other.

She hoped he hadn't forgotten her. And she wished she could let him know in some way that didn't make her seem too foolish that she wanted them to be friends again. But what could she say?

Of course! It was New Year's Eve. She could invite him to their apartment after the concert for a small impromptu party. Aunt Vi, Craig and Cindy, and perhaps a few others at the apartment building who didn't have other plans. Maybe she would even invite Mr. Denny.

As Diana came up to the door of Chris' dressing room, she heard voices and laughter from inside. The door was standing open and all at once she began to tremble from an acute attack of nerves. How could she approach Chris when he wasn't alone? Could she invite him to a party in those circumstances? Maybe he already had plans for after the concert. And was she truly certain she wanted to do this?

If she did start dating Chris, was she ready for all that could mean? She wasn't ready to trust completely again. But she was ready to make a new start, and it seemed her favorite gospel singer was the only man capable of helping her do that. In fact, he was the one making her *want* to do that!

When Diana stepped into the doorway of Chris' room, she was remembering the quartet's victory at the Gospel Quartet Convention in Nashville the previous October. They had won the Fan Award for favorite gospel quartet for the fourth year in a row. And Chris had once again been voted most popular lead singer. *Little wonder,* she thought, *with his voice and personality and dedication.* It was this she had on her mind when she paused to take in the scene before her and perhaps that was why it took her a moment to put an interpretation on what she saw.

It took only a few seconds after that for her to return swiftly, silently down the hall. What she had witnessed hadn't actually shocked her as much as the tear she caught escaping down her cheek when she at last got back to the lobby.

Chapter Sixteen _____

It snowed New Year's Day, Briarton's first snowfall of the year, and it had been a heavy one. A layer of white still covered most of the lawns in Briar Ridge, but now, almost a week later, everything seemed back to normal. Cindy had resumed school after the holiday break and Diana's college classes would begin in another week.

At the kitchen table she had begun her morning prayer and devotions as soon as Cindy left to catch her bus; but it seemed each time she examined a Scripture or tried to talk to the Lord, the scene in Chris' dressing room paraded on the screen of her mind in a drama she was unwilling to remember but couldn't make herself forget.

Why did it still matter after these several days? It wasn't as if she were in love with Chris Jarrett.

Cindy had wanted to know exactly what had occurred backstage, but Diana had managed to hold her off until the conclusion of the concert and Craig had walked them home. It had been hard enough to watch Chris on stage and listen to his touching music without having to explain why she felt like crying instead of rejoicing. She had scarcely heard the message of victory in his spendid songs, even when the quartet sang some of her favorites. After the concert she couldn't get away from the auditorium quickly enough.

"Tell me what happened," Cindy had burst out as soon as they stepped into the living room. "Was Chris glad to see you? I know he was."

"He didn't see me."

"I thought you were gonna talk to him. Wouldn't he talk to you? Is he mad?"

"He looked pretty happy to me."

When Diana had walked up to the open door of Chris' dressing room, the tall, broad-shouldered singer had stood with his back to her and his arm draped casually around the waist of a slender blonde woman. They had been laughing and talking in a familiar, intimate way, and if Diana had thought there was a chance Chris might still be interested in her she had abandoned that foolish notion on the spot.

Following Diana's explanation of all this, Cindy said loyally, "She might not be his girl friend."

"No, she was probably his mother."

"Or his sister."

"Chris doesn't have a sister and you know it."

"So? She might be the wife of someone in the group. Or she could just be a fan."

"He had his arm around her, Cindy, and they were talking like they'd known each other a *long* time."

"Maybe they have. She could still be a fan."

"Whoever she is, Chris obviously likes her. So can we please stop talking about it?"

"What if you're wrong, Diana? Chris told me he doesn't have a girl friend."

"He has one now. An old flame he's rekindled, I'd guess."

"But what if she isn't his girl friend? Don't you think you should find out for sure?"

"How am I going to do that? Call him up and say, 'Oh, by the way, Chris, that blonde you were holding the other night in your dressing room, she *is* your mother, isn't she?' "

"Well, you could," Cindy said, barely stifling a giggle.

"What I'm going to do is forget all about Christopher Jarrett," she said firmly. "You can't trust men," she added more to herself than to Cindy. "About the time you get ready to give them all your attention, they go off and find someone else."

"If you wait too long to let them know how you feel," Cindy finished for her.

"I'll be waiting even longer from now on."

"I think you should try to talk to Chris one more time."

"Well, I'm not."

"I can."

"You do and I'll forget I'm your sister and I'll turn you over my knee like I would if I were Mother."

"You wouldn't dare!"

"Cindy, promise me you won't try to talk to him," Diana said disconsolately.

"Sure I'll talk to him. What do you expect me to do, ignore him?"

"You know what I mean. Don't talk about me. Or that woman I saw him with." When Cindy made no comment, Diana said, "Do you promise?"

Cindy slid one hand behind her back. Was there really any truth in that old saying that if you made a promise and crossed your fingers while you were making it you didn't have to keep it? "I promise," she smiled.

• • •

Diana opened her sketch pad. She was curled up in the chair by the stereo working on the homework assignment for one of her art classes. It was a Friday night and she was doing a study of eyes and noses. With pencil in hand, she began to draw a pair of eyes. When they were finished, she colored them blue. The bluest blue she had ever seen. She shaped a nose then, long and narrow and straight. She filled in a wide forehead and cheekbones far apart. Next she added a tender, shapely mouth, a firm jawline and a square, determined chin. Around the face she sketched hair, soft honey-brown hair, and when she had finished the drawing she sat staring at a picture of Chris Jarrett.

When the buzzer sounded at the door, Diana guiltily flipped the cover on her pad and placed it on the stereo. At the door she greeted her aunt.

"I've been over checking on Mr. Denny," she said, stalking

heavily into the room. "I hadn't seen him all day and I was getting worried."

"Is he sick?" Diana asked and took a place beside her aunt on the loveseat.

"It's his back. He says it's hurt him so much today he can't get up and down. I told him if he didn't go to the doctor right away he'd be sorry."

"Can I go over and do anything for him?"

"No, he's doing all right now. I took him up some supper. But he's hardly able to walk around tonight, I hope he'll see reason now about going to the doctor."

Later, when Cindy came in from visiting with Beth, Diana made a point of telling her about Mr. Denny. "Do you think you could go over and check on him before you go to bed? I've really got a lot of homework to get done tonight."

Diana felt her sister stiffen slightly. "I don't think there's anything I could do for him."

Diana bit back a sharp retort. Better not to push, she decided. "Well, maybe tomorrow you could take him over some lunch or something."

•   •   •

Cindy was standing just inside the door at the drugstore in the shopping plaza when suddenly she felt someone's hand grip her arm.

To her gasp of surprise, he said, "Who are you waiting for, little lady?"

"Chris!"

"Are you by yourself, honey?"

"I'm waiting for Beth and Corey. We were ready to leave when they remembered something they forgot and went back to get it."

Chris moved out of the doorway, glancing toward the rows of booths and the soda fountain off to their right. "Why don't we get a Coke while you're waiting for them?" he suggested, and still holding Cindy's arm he guided her over to a padded booth in the corner.

"Beth and Corey won't know where I am," she said, as they slid into seats across from each other.

"I can see the aisle to the door from here," he said. "I'll watch for them."

"Do you know what they look like?"

"Sure, you've introduced them to me at the auditorium."

"What are you doing here, Chris?"

"I've been over at Billy's. The group's been rehearsing. I just stopped by on my way home to pick up a few things for the road."

"Are you getting ready to go on a tour?"

"We're always going somewhere," he said with a sigh.

A waitress in a blue-and-white striped dressed and starched apron came to take their order. When Chris had asked for two large Cokes, he addressed Cindy, "Did you want anything else?"

"No. Thanks."

He smiled at the waitress. "That's all."

She lingered a moment, returning his smile hopefully, then moved on.

"How've you been?" Chris said. "I haven't seen you for a while."

"I've been just fine. I've been to two of your concerts at the auditorium but I didn't get a chance to talk to you."

"How's school?"

"Okay. I'm taking chorus now."

"I'm glad to hear that. I want you to use your voice under a competent director. In a few more years you should begin voice lessons."

"I'm going to a Valentine Banquet week after next," she said. "The youth group at church is having it."

"Cindy-rella going to a ball, huh?"

"Craig Jarvis asked me to go."

"Complete with handsome prince. Is he the boy who stares at you?"

Cindy giggled. "It's not really a date or anything. Well, in a way it is, I guess. But there'll be lots of chaperones there."

When the waitress brought their Cokes, Chris took a big swallow of his and sat gazing across the table at Cindy for a quiet moment. Finally, he said, "How's Diana?"

"Oh, she's fine. She's—"

When the girl didn't go on, Chris said, "She's what?"

"Oh nothing, She's just fine like I said. She's home working on some layouts for Marshall's."

After another silent scrutiny of his companion, Chris said, "Is there anything wrong, honey?"

"No."

"You don't sound too sure about that."

"I'm sure. Only . . ."

"Only what?"

"Well . . . if you make a promise to somebody, but . . . well, did you ever not want to make a promise, but somebody made you anyway?"

"Not that I can recall. But I might have."

"Well, if you made this promise, but you never intended to keep it, is it all right to break it?"

"If you made a promise you shouldn't break it."

"But if I was forced to make it."

"Then it might depend on the circumstances. Is there anything you think you should tell me?"

"Yes, but I can't."

"Diana doesn't want you to?"

"Yeah."

"Then you'd better not."

"You can ask her."

"Diana doesn't want me to ask her anything."

"Oh, yes—" Cindy stopped.

But Chris had heard enough. "You mean she's changed her mind about me? Why hasn't she let me know? I thought I made it plain that all she had to do was tell me."

"She tried."

"What do you mean?" To the silence that followed his question, Chris said, "Maybe you'd better tell me the whole story, honey."

"Diana will kill me if I do."

He smiled then. "I'll take full responsibility for corrupting your integrity. And I won't let her *kill* you."

"I will tell you this. Diana hasn't changed her mind about you."

"But you just said—"

"She's liked you all along. Well, almost from the first."

"Don't kid me, honey. I've been about as popular with her as an all-over case of poison ivy."

"I told you, she's afraid. She's afraid she'll get hurt again."

"I understand the feeling."

"Why don't you go talk to her?"

"You haven't told me the rest of it."

Cindy shrugged her slender shoulders. "I guess I might as well. Maybe Diana won't kill me too dead." With the sound of Chris' soft laughter in her ears, Cindy went on, "Diana came to see you at the auditorium New Year's Eve."

"What do you mean she came to see me?"

"She went backstage. To your dressing room. She wanted to tell you she liked you, or missed you, or something. I don't know what she was going to say exactly. Anyway she came to see you."

"She didn't come to my dressing room. I never saw her at all New Year's Eve. I haven't seen her since before Christmas, the night I gave you the Bible."

"Oh, I've been reading it a lot."

"Great. But what about New Year's Eve?"

"Diana said she came to your dressing room. She said she saw you and...and somebody."

"Saw me and who?"

"This is the part I'm really not supposed to tell."

"You've got to tell me, Cindy. Who did Diana—wait a minute. Did she see me with a pretty blonde girl?"

"She said you had your arm around her and you all were laughing and talking. She thought—"

"Never mind. I know what she thought." Chris took a drink of his Coke before he let out a shout of laughter.

"Diana didn't think it was so funny," said Cindy. "Is that blonde girl your new girl friend? Diana thought she seemed more like an *old* girl friend."

"She's our piano player's wife. I've known her a long time. We went to college together."

"Then you...I mean you..."

"Still like Diana? You bet! I've been hoping and praying something would happen. I've missed her like crazy!"

At the apartment house behind the shopping plaza, Chris mounted the stairs whistling to himself and climbing two steps at a time. In the hallway he rang the buzzer of apartment number five. When Diana opened the door, he said, "Hello, Angel."

Chapter Seventeen _____

A light snow began to fall the day before the Valentine Banquet. For a while it looked as if Briarton would get more snow than had originally been predicted. But as Cindy dressed that February evening the thick clouds had cleared and the rich blackness of the sky was studded with a splendor of stars.

Cindy had on a brilliant red dress with three-quarter sleeves and semi-scooped neckline. Diana had helped arrange her long hair in curls on top of her head. Cindy was fastening tiny pearl earrings in her ears when Diana entered her bedroom.

"What about my face?" she said to her sister. "Do you think I should wear a little makeup?"

"You have the kind of beauty that will never need much makeup. Your complexion is clear as rain. Makeup would only clutter it. But maybe tonight with that red dress you could wear a little blusher."

"And some eye shadow?"

"Sure."

"Will you put it on for me?"

When Diana had set the finishing touches to Cindy's face, she stood back admiring her sister's sweet, delicate beauty. "You'll be the loveliest girl at the banquet."

"Do I really look pretty? I sure wish I could see myself."

A great stab of pain wrenched Diana's heart, but she was saved from having to make some empty, comforting comment when the buzzer sounded at the door.

"That must be Craig!" said Cindy excitedly.

"It might be Chris."

"That's right. I forgot he's taking you out to dinner tonight." Cindy gave her sister a smile of triumphant satisfaction. "Ain't you glad I broke my promise?"

"Yes, but..."

"But what? Is something wrong? What has Chris done now?"

Laughing, Diana started for the door. "Nothing. He's wonderful. Only..."

"Only you're not sure of him, right?"

"I don't know."

"Diana, you've got to forget what Glen did."

"I'm trying." *Dear Lord, how I'm trying,* she thought. And maybe that trust would come soon.

"What double good fortune I have tonight," the singer said when Diana let him in. "I have two adorable ladies to take out."

"I'm not going out with you and Diana!" Cindy quickly protested. "I'm going to the banquet with Craig."

"Oh, that's right," said Chris in a humorous pretense. "Cindy-rella is going to the ball."

"That's *Cinderella.*"

"And so, Cinderella, where's your handsome prince?"

She smiled mischievously. "Would you be my prince, Chris?"

"Not me. I'm much too plain for that role."

"Yeah. Sure. And their ain't no cows in Texas."

They laughed and Diana said, "There *aren't* any cows in Texas."

Chris gave each of the girls a big red box, shaped like a heart and made of satin and lace.

"If I eat all this candy I'll be too fat to fit in my new dress," Cindy said.

They laughed again, and while the girls were thanking Chris for their gifts Craig arrived. After Diana offered him a few motherly statements about walking Cindy home from church as soon as the banquet was over, Cindy and Craig left.

As Chris and Diana drove in silence to the restaurant, the singer inquired, "What's on your mind, Angel?" and reached over to take hold of her hand.

"I was thinking about Cindy. Do you think I'll ever stop feeling sorry for her? I mean, sorry about her blindness?"

"How could you be human and not be sorry she's blind?"

She faced him. "Oh, Chris, how *can* God let her be blind?"

"Cindy and I talked about that. But I don't pretend to have all the answers, except like I told her, how could God have prevented the accident and still have given us free wills?"

After a silence, Diana remarked, "She's accepting her blindness a lot better now. I know it's God working in her life, but He used you to do that. I can never thank you enough for that."

His eyes steadied on the road, Chris said, "Is that the only reason you're going out with me now?"

Diana flashed him a stormy look. "Of course not!" In a minute she said, "You don't really think that, do you?"

"No."

"Cindy's singing in the youth choir again. Has she told you?" He nodded and she continued, "Do you really think her voice is good enough to train?"

"Yes, I do. She has real possibilities."

"That's a blessing, isn't it? Being blind won't keep her from developing her talent."

"What do you think of her friend Craig?"

"He's mature for his age in a lot of ways. Of course, they *are* just friends. They're so young yet. But he's sincere about how he feels toward Cindy, I think."

"I'm sincere in how I feel about her sister, too," he said, taking his eyes briefly from the road to smile at her.

"Are you, Chris?"

He squeezed her hand. "Don't trust me yet, do you?"

"Well, I did find you with another woman in your arms."

"It was hardly like that. Anyway, I told you who she was."

"I know."

"I guess you think I fool around with the guys' wives?"

"Don't be silly!"

"How's Mr. Denny doing?" Chris said, bringing up a new topic.

"He's not doing well. And he still won't see a doctor. You know what I think? Aunt Vi and I were talking about it the other day. Mr. Denny blames himself for Cindy's blindness, just the way she does. And I wonder if he feels so guilty he just doesn't care anymore."

"I see what you mean. Maybe he doesn't even care enough about himself to go to a doctor. I've heard of people letting guilt feelings eat away at them until they don't care anymore."

"Did Cindy tell you she invited Mr. Denny for Christmas dinner with Aunt Vi and all of us?"

"No."

"But she really wasn't that friendly to him Christmas Day."

"Still, that was a start toward forgiving him."

"You've talked to her about that, haven't you?"

"We talked a little."

"I asked her to go over and check on him one day when he was feeling really bad, but she never did."

"Give her more time, Angel. More time."

• • •

Cindy was in the kitchen rummaging through the refrigerator when she heard footsteps on the stairs. She slammed the door shut and hurried into the living room as Diana and Chris came in.

"I smell pizza," the girl said.

"That's right," Diana said, taking a large, flat box from Chris and starting for the kitchen.

"Is that Chris with you?" Cindy asked.

As she was about to answer, Diana glanced at the singer. He placed a finger to his lips in a gesture of silence. Then he winked.

"What makes you think there's somebody with me?" Diana said, joining in his game.

"I heard two sets of footsteps."

"You must have been mistaken."

"Oh, you're teasing me," Cindy said, moving toward the door. "Somebody came in with you. It's Chris, ain't it?"

"You don't know if it's Chris or not. You'll just have to guess."

"No, I don't. I can tell if it's Chris." She reached out and touched his coat sleeve. Then she felt for his hand. Carefully, she traced the shape of his little finger. "Oh, Chris, it is you!"

He burst into laughter. "I'm marked for life by crooked fingers," he said. "O, God, why did You curse me so?"

"So you couldn't play tricks on blind girls," came Cindy's retort.

"I give up," the singer said, "I can't hide from you."

"I was just letting you have your fun," she said. "I knew it was you all along."

"How? No, don't tell me. Let me guess. You smelled my after-shave."

"You sure wear enough of it."

He laughed deeply and ruffled her hair. "I should be ashamed for teasing you, Cinderella."

"Oh, that's okay. I don't really care if you tease me. You can do anything you want."

Chris gazed quietly at her for a moment, absorbing the adoration he heard in her sweet voice. Unexpectedly he reached out and took her hands. "You know something, sweetheart, I don't think I've ever met anybody who makes me feel good the way you do. It's the way you accept me just as I am. You know, Cindy, that's how God loves us—with His unconditional love. He loves us as we are—good and bad. And it's an absolute love. It's forever and nothing can change it."

"That's how I feel about you, all right," Cindy said. "But how did you know?"

"I can feel it, honey. Sometimes things don't have to be said."

Chris glanced at Diana then. She had set out the pizza on the table and had taken plates and glasses from the cabinet. She was standing by the table now, staring at him with an unreadable expression on her face.

He had wanted an opportunity to get to know her, Diana reminded herself, and having been given that chance, she hoped he was not disappointed. The only problem still, she decided ruefully, was her feelings for him. Could he make her forget the past? Could he win her trust, and finally, her heart? Would she ever love him the way she knew he was growing to love her?

Chapter Eighteen _____

Easter Sunday came during the middle of April when grass had just begun to turn green and trees were decorated anew with tiny buds. It was a day of cloudless, sun-filled skies, and Cindy and Diana dressed for church in pretty pastel dresses they had shopped for at Marshall's the previous week.

Before Chris arrived Cindy addressed her sister in an excited tone. "Are you nervous about meeting Chris' mom and dad?"

"A little. But I'm sure I'll like them."

"To have a son like Chris they must be pretty special people."

Following the morning service at the small country church Chris and his family attended, the singer drove the girls back to the farm for dinner with his parents. The brick farmhouse was set back off the road and nestled comfortably among giant maple and sycamore trees. Near the house ran a narrow, gurgling creek, over which was built a small bridge of flat stones and pebbles.

Mr. Jarrett was tall and wide-shouldered like his son. He had a large, becoming smile and familiar blue eyes that harbored an appearance of vivaciousness despite his recent heart attack.

Mrs. Jarrett was an attractive, slender woman with a more quiet personality than either her husband or her son, but she made Diana and Cindy feel so much at home in her subdued kind of way that both girls warmed to her immediately.

The atmosphere in the Jarrett home, one of casual comfort and old-fashioned hospitality, abounded in the country kitchen at the back of the house. Diana fell in love with the old-brick fireplace at one end of the room, with cozy wing chairs flanking each side of the hearth. In the center of the kitchen area was a wooden table with Windsor chairs cushioned in blue gingham that matched the fabric of the wing chairs.

Mrs. Jarrett served country ham, green beans, and candied yams on porcelain china with a blue border. Following a lengthy, casual meal, Chris sent his parents and Cindy out to the back porch while Diana and he washed the dishes. Later, when the last dish had been dried and put away, they joined them, taking seats side by side on the wooden swing at one end of the porch.

It wasn't long until Mr. Jarrett excused himself to walk down to the barn and check on a new calf, and Mrs. Jarrett took Cindy back inside to inspect a quilt she was making.

Chris was laughing softly as the back door closed on them. "Everybody sure made a quick getaway."

"You're parents are so nice, Chris," Diana said, smiling. "I really like them." When he took her hand she said, "Your mother's so much quieter than you and your dad."

"Would you believe Daddy's a lot quieter now than he was before his heart attack?"

"He seems so outgoing now."

"He used to be mouthier than I am."

"I guess between you and your dad," she said with a laugh, "your mother doesn't have much of a chance to talk."

"She's quieter by nature than we are. But she's not reserved when you get to know her real well. She tells Dad and I what she thinks, all right. She's really been our support over the years. The homebody type. She's never really cared for traveling, although she used to go with Daddy on the road until I came along later and put a stop to that. I went with them until I started school. I think Mom was really glad to stay home then."

"I'm surpised she didn't have lots of children to stay home with."

"They wanted more, but I was all they could have." He chuckled suddenly. "At least that's what they told me. Probably the truth is they took one look at me and decided they didn't want to make any more messes like that."

When Diana stopped laughing, she said, "Oh, Chris, Cindy's right. You are nothing but a tease."

"Mom and Dad kept foster children until a few years ago. Right after they married and had me they were too poor to adopt or I'm sure they would have. I think Mom misses having kids around."

In a moment Chris let go of Diana's hand and slid his arm around her shoulders. "I'm so glad you could spend this day with my family. You really make the day complete for me."

He pulled her into his arms then and Diana lifted her face for a kiss of exquisite tenderness.

"I'm in love with you, Angel. You know that, don't you?"

"Oh, Chris, I . . . I care for you more than I can say. I just don't know if it's love. Yet."

"It's all right. I understand. I love you, but I don't want to rush you. I can wait. For a while."

• • •

Sunday morning two weeks later when Chris arrived at the girls' apartment to accompany them to church, he was smiling proudly as he strode into the living room. "Marlene had her baby last night!" he announced. "It's a healthy nine-pound boy."

He took the girls to visit Marlene and Billy and the baby on a warm evening in early May. In the lemon and white nursery, Cindy lingered after the others had gone back to the living room, talking quietly to Marlene as she rocked the baby in a beechwood rocker.

"Would you like to hold little Mike?" Marlene said to the girl after a while.

Cindy was curled up on a fluffy yellow rug in the middle of the floor. "Are you sure it's okay?" she said rising.

Marlene got up from the rocking chair and Cindy sat down. "He's not nearly as fragile as you might think," the baby's mother said as she placed him in the curve of Cindy's arm.

The girl cuddled the infant close to her bosom. "He sure is tiny. I wish I could see him. Chris says he looks like you."

"He does, but I think he favors his daddy, too."

"He's sleeping, isn't he? His breathing is real regular." Cindy was quiet for a few minutes, cuddling the baby and rocking him gently. "Do you think I'll ever get married and have a baby?"

Marlene sat on a padded bench near the baby's bed. "Yes, I think so. When you're a little older."

"Do you think I'll marry someone who's blind?"

"I don't know. Do you think you want to?"

"I haven't thought much about it. I've got a lot of time. Do you think Chris and Diana will get married?"

Marlene smiled a smile Cindy couldn't see. "I think if Chris has his way about it they will."

"Chris said he almost got married one time. I guess he was teasing."

"He probably wished he was."

"Why?"

"Because it turned out to be a pretty terrible thing."

"What happened?"

"He was engaged to a girl from a real well-to-do family. About three weeks before the wedding she ran off with some rich guy who had come down here from Canada. It all happened about two years before his daddy's heart attack. Everybody was talking about it. They said the guy was French and good-looking, a real hunk like Chris, they said."

"Why did she go off with that other guy? How could she give up Chris for *anybody*?"

"I don't know. She was a beautiful girl, and she was used to the better things, and there was a lot of talk after they left about how wealthy the guy was. Of course, Chris isn't *that* rich." Marlene paused. "The whole thing was really hard on Chris. In fact, he was downright humiliated. There was a picture in the local paper of the ring this guy gave her. It was a big thing. And you know, she never did give back the ring Chris gave her. But if I know our Chris, he wouldn't have wanted her to. Whenever I think about it, I sure feel sorry for him.

He was so hurt. His heart was broken. I know if it hadn't been for his faith in Jesus he'd never have gotten over it.''

"The same thing happened to Diana," Cindy said. "Her boyfriend broke off their engagement, too. He went back to his old girl friend. I don't know if Diana will ever forget what he did. Marlene, do you think Chris has forgotten about that other girl?"

"I don't know if you ever really forget someone you've loved, but I think Chris is over his love for her. I think that must have happened about the time he met your sister.''

• • •

Diana drew her umbrella to a close and gave it a brisk shake. She looked up as Aunt Vi came down the stairs. "It sure is wet out there," she said.

"Maybe it'll stop by the time you have to go back out to work."

"I hope so. How's Mr. Denny?"

"He's resting now. I'm going to take him up some supper later."

Behind them the front door opened and Chris came in, pausing to shake the rain from his hair and clothes. When he saw Diana and her aunt he smiled. "Think it'll rain soon?"

They laughed as he came to Diana's side and brushed her cheek with a kiss.

"Mmm, you smell good," she said. "Did you just step out of the shower?"

"I sure did," he laughed.

"Did you break the bottle?"

He sent her a quizzical glance.

"The bottle of after shave lotion. The way you smell you must have spilled the whole thing on you."

Chris grinned boyishly at Aunt Vi and slipped an arm around Diana. "Your niece is a smart-aleck, Aunt Vi. She's nothing but a smart-aleck."

"I'm sure you can keep her in line, Chris."

"I'm sure willing to try," he said, gazing down at Diana,

a look of love in his bright eyes.

"Mr. Denny came home from the hospital today," Diana told the singer.

"That's good news."

It had been in desperation that Aunt Vi finally called her family doctor. She had gone up to check on the handyman one evening and found him in so much pain he couldn't get out of bed. When the doctor learned of his fall just before the Christmas holidays, he had ordered him to the hospital at once. After X-rays were taken it was determined that Mr. Denny had fractured two of the vertebrae in his lower back. In addition, the doctor said, that in the risk Mr. Denny had been unknowingly taking, it was a miracle the fractured vertebraes hadn't pinched the spinal cord and caused paralysis.

"Cindy's been helping Aunt Vi take care of the plants," Diana said. "But I never could get her to visit Mr. Denny in the hospital."

"You mean that old guy was in the hospital three weeks and she didn't go see him even once?" asked Chris incredulously. When Diana shook her head, he said, "Since I've been gone so much lately, we haven't had a good heart-to-heart for a while. I think I better have another talk with that little lady."

"Would you, Chris?" Diana said. "I'm afraid she's still carrying an awful grudge against him."

Chris took the girls out for supper that night and then dropped Diana off at Marshall's. It had quit raining by this time and instead of taking Cindy back to the apartment he headed his car out Franklin Highway away from Briar Ridge.

"Where are we going?" she asked shortly.

"I thought we'd go for a drive. There's a roadside park a few miles out past the turnoff to the farm. We could go out there for a while. We'll come back and get Diana when she gets off."

"What are we going to do at the park?"

"I thought we could go out there where it's quiet and just talk."

To Chris' surprise Cindy was silent for the rest of the drive, and when they reached the small park he pulled into a shady area near a group of picnic tables and outdoor grills.

"Do you want to get out and walk around? Maybe sit down? I suppose the grass is awfully wet, though. And the tables, too."

Seeming to ignore his remarks, Cindy said. "What did you want to talk about, Chris?"

"What makes you think I have anything special in mind?"

"You forget. I'm blind. But I can read you in other ways. I always know when you've got something on your mind. Just like Diana."

"In that case, I guess you know what I'm thinking."

"I'm not exactly a mind reader, but I think I know what you want to talk about."

When she didn't go on, Chris said, "Are you going to tell me?"

"You're the one who wants to talk."

"All right," he said, clamping down firmly on his sudden irritation. "Tell me why you didn't go to the hospital to see Mr. Denny."

"Why should I go to the hospital? I helped Aunt Vi take care of his ol' plants."

"Why did you ask him to have Christmas dinner with your family?"

"I didn't exactly ask him. Anyway, he always eats Christmas dinner with us."

"You really haven't forgiven him for what happened, have you?"

"I don't know."

"When he fell down the steps, he was taking a big chance with his back by not seeing a doctor. He could have been crippled for the rest of his life, did you know that? But I don't think he cared."

"I don't understand."

"I think he would have, if he thought you cared a little. He blames himself for your blindness, mostly because *you* blame him. He won't be able to forgive himself until you forgive him. Maybe not even then."

"So?"

"Cindy, you'll never become the Christian God wants you to be until you get this bitterness out of your heart."

"I've been trying. Whether you believe me or not."

"I believe you."

"Then leave me alone. I'll work it out."

"How?"

"I don't know!" she stormed unexpectedly. "It's easy for you to talk. You can see. You can do anything. You don't have to spend your life in the gray shadows. You don't know what it's like!"

Before Cindy realized it, great tears had escaped from her eyes and were streaming down her cheeks. Chris looked over at her and somewhere in the depths of his soul he felt a great stab of pain. When he put his arm around her, she turned and wept into his shoulder. "I didn't know you could be so mean," she sobbed. "I thought you were the nicest person in the world."

"I'm not mean, little one. But sometimes the circumstances of life call for us to be tough."

"That's not love. I thought you cared about me."

"That's tough love, honey. A Christian's love has to be tough because that's how God's love is. That's the only way it can be."

In a minute Cindy sat up and Chris took out his handkerchief and began wiping her face. "Feel better now?"

"Do you?" she accused.

"I didn't mean to make you cry. It tears me apart. I'm sorry."

"I forgive you."

"Just like that? Why?"

"Because I love you, that's why. You know that."

"I hurt you and you forgive me. That's tough love. Don't you love Mr. Denny?" he added.

"Not anymore."

"I thought you told me you were a Christian."

"I am."

"Christian love is enduring."

"No matter how much it hurts?"

"It hurt Jesus to love us. It cost Him His life. If He hadn't been hurt—rejected—we couldn't have salvation. It took a radical cure—His blood—for a radical disease—sin."

"So?"

"The love of Jesus could turn your bitterness toward Mr. Denny into something of beauty—forgiveness—just like an oyster turns a grain of sand into a beautiful pearl."

"How do you mean?"

"A precious pearl is caused by something that gets inside the oyster's shell and hurts or irritates it. The mantle, on the inside of the oyster, is smooth and has a silvery pearl sheen. It produces layer after layer of this pearly material around the grain of sand until finally, after several years, a lustrous pearl is formed. But something that's a lot more precious than a pearl is your relationship with Mr. Denny."

It was a while before Cindy spoke. "Chris, do you think I can make what happened to me into a pearl?"

"I know you can, sweetheart. With God's help, I know you can."

Chapter Nineteen _____

A few days later Chris sat talking about his work with Diana and Cindy in the living room of their apartment. "We'll be doing a lot more concerts this summer than we've done during the winter," he said. "We'll be doing more revivals and a lot of fairs."

"We miss you so much when you're gone," Cindy said on a wistful note.

"Maybe you two can go with us sometime." He glanced at Diana seated beside him on the couch. "What about this Sunday? We're doing a revival at a church in Mapleton Sunday morning and another one that night."

"But do you have room for us in your bus?" Cindy asked.

"Sure. The guys bring their wives along all the time."

The following Sunday the big silver bus with *The Jarretts Quartet* painted on each side in red letters whizzed along the highway south of Briar Ridge toward the town of Mapleton fifty miles away. At a large church off the main thoroughfare the popular quartet flooded the sanctuary with songs of love and praise to God. That evening on the other side of town at an old-time tent revival meeting the quartet's beautiful harmony brought peace and joy to many and shared the Good News of Jesus in its own unique way.

"Chris, I've never had so much fun!" Cindy said as they loaded the bus for the trip home that night. "How can we thank you for taking us?"

"You can go again some time. We love to sing for the Lord and make people happy."

"You were so good today," Diana told Chris. "I think you sounded better than I've ever heard you."

"We did get things right for a change," Chris said, smiling. "We even got lucky a couple times and we all ended together."

Chris turned to Billy and the piano player sitting in the seat behind them. "Billy even got the words right."

"And you sang all the songs just the way we planned them—for a change," the tenor quipped.

Cindy spoke up. "What's your favorite gospel song, Chris?"

"That's a tough question, Cinderella," he replied. "My favorite kind of music is the old Negro spirituals of years and years ago."

"Don't you have one gospel song you like more than any other?"

"Just one? Well, if I had to pick only one song, I suppose it would have to be one of the best loved gospel songs of all time—'How Great Thou Art.' "

"I like that one too," said Cindy. "I guess just about everybody does. But my favorite is 'Peace in the Valley,' that you sang for me on my birthday. You know why it's my favorite? It was the first gospel song I ever heard you sing." She smiled adoringly across the aisle at him.

When they got back to the apartment house, Chris came upstairs to say good night to the girls. After Cindy excused herself to get ready for bed, he lingered at the door with Diana.

"Did you have a nice time today, Angel?" he asked, enfolding her in his arms and drawing her near. *How good it feels to be so close to him,* Diana thought. *Didn't she always want him to hold her this way?*

"I really did. I haven't done much traveling, but I think I'd like it."

"I wish you could go with me all the time. I suppose it'll sound crazy if I tell you this, but sometimes when we're driving along I get to wondering what you're doing and if you're all right. I just get to thinking about you, more than at other times. I sound like a nut, don't I?"

For a moment Diana was lost in his tender gaze. "Do you really think about me so much?"

"All the time. You know, sweetheart, I couldn't be happier than I am now. Singing for the Lord and helping Daddy with the farm and being with you makes me the happiest man in the world."

He bent and kissed her with deep emotion and Diana's heart pounded out of control. There could be no denying Chris' love for her, and she was just as sure she was beginning to return his love. But if that were true then why did she still have these niggling doubts? Why was she still afraid to trust him?

• • •

Diana's college graduation exercises came during the third week of May. Chris insisted on taking off that night when the quartet journeyed to a nearby town.

"How can they sing without you?" Cindy wanted to know.

Chris only laughed. "They'll do just fine, Cinderella. Just fine. One of our guitar players can fill in for me."

"*Nobody* can fill in for you!"

A week after graduation Diana went for an interview with the public relations office at the local seminary. There would be an opening in the fall. Upon seeing examples of the work from her portfolio, the department manager had assured her she stood every chance of qualifying for the job.

The girls were finishing supper later, when across the table Cindy said, "I sure miss Chris, don't you?"

"Yes. But he'll be home in another week."

"At least we get to talk to him on the phone," Cindy said. "He must be spending a fortune on phone calls. Diana, when do you think you all will get married?"

Startled, Diana took a minute to answer. "You're taking a lot for granted. Chris hasn't asked me yet."

"He will soon, I bet. I know how much he loves you. I can hear it in the tone of his voice."

"And what do you hear in my voice?"

"Oh, you love him, too."

"You're sure?"

"Aren't you?"

"Yes...I guess so."

"You guess so! Diana, is something wrong?" When her sister made no comment, Cindy said, "You couldn't possibly be thinking about Glen *now* could you?"

"I've told you, I never think about Glen."

"Just what he *did*. Diana, what does Chris have to do to prove to you he's not like Glen?"

"I don't know. I wish I did."

"I may not be as old as you are, and I don't guess I really know anything about it yet, but somehow I know if you really love Chris you'll trust him, too. I just know that love and trust have to go together."

I know it too, thought Diana. *So maybe I don't love Chris after all....*

• • •

Cindy rang the buzzer and waited. When finally no sound came from inside the apartment, she opened the door slowly and called out. "Mr. Denny? Are you awake, Mr. Denny?"

"Cindy? Is that you, Cindy?" His tone held surprise mingled with joy.

"Is it all right if I come in?"

"Come back here, child, I'm in the bedroom."

Cindy made her way through the apartment she remembered as well as her own. Inside the bedroom door she paused. It was a minute or two before she spoke again. "How are you, Mr. Denny?"

"I'm lots better, Cindy. But the doctor says I still have to rest every day."

"But your back's not hurting you like before?"

"It's better now."

"I've been helping Aunt Vi look after everything."

"She told me you were helping with the plants. I guess I'll be getting out of this bed more after I go back to the doctor next week."

"I'm—...I'm awful sorry you got hurt, Mr. Denny."

"Why don't you pull up a chair, Cindy, and sit down."

"No...I...I just came over to see how you were. I'm sorry I ain't been over before."

"You don't have nothing to be sorry for, child. I'm the one—"

"No. It's...it's all right."

The old man could scarcely believe his ears. "I don't blame you if you hate me."

"I don't hate you. Anyway...not anymore."

"But it was my fault. I was driving. I..."

"Maybe it was your fault. Maybe it wasn't. I've been thinking a lot about it. I've been praying about it. And we can't go back. And that part's not all right. But we can't change what happened."

"I'd give anything if I could."

"You can't. And it only makes it worse to blame somebody for what you can't change. You gotta be tough, Mr. Denny. That's what Chris said. He's Diana's boyfriend. He said God's love is tough and a Christian has to have tough love, too."

A tear escaped the old man's eyes and traced a crooked path down his wrinkled cheek. "Cindy, I...I don't deserve...to be forgiven."

"I've been learning in my Bible class that nobody deserves to be forgiven for sin, but God forgives us because He loves us. Chris said that was called unconditional love."

When Mr. Denny didn't offer any comment, after a while Cindy said, "Aunt Vi says you ain't been going to church anymore."

"I haven't felt much like it, I guess."

"If you feel like it next Sunday, will you go with Diana and me?"

"You want me to?"

"Sure I want you to. I wouldn't be asking you if I didn't."

"I'm sure I'll feel lots better by next Sunday," the old man said brightly.

"I gotta be going now. I gotta help Aunt Vi. Now that school's out I got more time to help her till you're feeling better. You want anything before I go?"

"No, child. I can manage. I get up and down all right now. I'm supposed to be getting out everyday for a walk."

"Mr. Denny," Cindy said after a pause. "I was wondering if I could ask you something."

"What is it?"

"Do you suppose I could have the wandering jew back? I mean, I guess I don't deserve to have it, but I'd sorta like to keep it in my room again."

A smile broke into the old man's lined features. "I've been taking real good care of it for you."

Chapter Twenty _____

Cindy sat smiling on a row near the stage. On one side of her sat Diana and Aunt Vi. On the other side was Mr. Denny and Mr. and Mrs. McIntosh.

It had been enough of a surprise to Diana when Cindy came in that afternoon and announced that Mr. Denny was going to the Old-time Gospel Sing with them. She hadn't said anything about her little talk with the handyman the week before. But when Cindy and Mr. McIntosh had come carrying up the wandering jew to Cindy's room and when Mr. Denny had joined them for church on Sunday, Diana realized something of significance had taken place. Still, she hadn't questioned her sister, as difficult as it had been not to. Obviously Cindy had worked through her bitterness after Chris' last talk with her. And if she decided to discuss the details, Diana was more than ready to listen. If not, what really needed to be said after all? It was her outward actions that showed the inner change in her attitude, and Diana could only be grateful to God. And to Chris.

It had been Cindy's mention that afternoon of the McIntoshes that had truly startled her sister.

"I think I'll go down and invite Mr. and Mrs. McIntosh to the gospel concert tonight," Cindy said.

"They don't impress me as the kind who would enjoy a gospel concert. You know how they always complain about every little thing that goes on."

"Maybe that's one of the things wrong with the world, Diana.

Most of the time we take people like they seem. We don't bother to find out what they're really like deep inside. Maybe if we'd take time to really get to know people, we'd find out there are a lot more nice people around than we think."

This bit of unexpected wisdom from her little sister set Diana to thinking about the direction Cindy's life was taking. She smiled a joyous smile. Yes, Cindy was going to make it. She would be one of the victors, in spite of her handicap.

"Folks, we call ourselves performers," Chris said in his soft baritone, "and I know you've come here tonight to be entertained. But we aren't going to perform and we aren't just going to entertain. We came here tonight to sing about the love of Jesus. We want to share the gospel with you through some of His beautiful songs. Right now we'd like to sing a song for you that's loved by almost everyone—'How Great Thou Art.' "

The musicians began to play as Chris smiled and lifted his velvet tone on his special arrangement of the hymn:

> O Lord my God! when I in awesome wonder
> Consider all the worlds Thy hands have made,
> I see the stars, I hear the rolling thunder,
> Thy pow'r throughout the universe displayed,

The rest of the quartet joined him on the first part of the third verse:

> When Christ shall come with shout of acclamation
> And take me home, what joy shall fill my heart!

Chris finished the verse:

> Then I shall bow in humble adoration
> And there proclaim—my God—how great Thou art!

The group blended their harmony for the chorus:

> Then sings my soul, my Savior God to Thee;
> How great Thou art! How great Thou art!
> Then sings my soul, my Savior God to Thee;
> How great Thou art! How great Thou art!

"Everybody join in!" Chris invited, and the gathering rose and a volume of voices filled the auditorium with the chorus.

The next morning Chris picked up the girls and took them to church with him and then to the farm for dinner and a leisurely afternoon. It would be one of the few free Sundays he would have all summer, Chris had pointed out to Diana, and she couldn't hide her joy at being with him and his family at these special times.

After dinner in the comfortable old kitchen, Chris and Diana washed the dishes for his mother before they stole away from the family for a quiet walk along the creek. With her hand in his, Chris guided Diana beside the rushing brook until they came to a clump of trees grouped together to form a semicircle near the bank. In the shade of the oak trees he pulled her close for a long, gentle kiss.

When they parted he gazed deeply into her eyes. "You look very happy today," he said.

"Only because I am."

"Is there any special reason why you're so happy?"

"It's just this place, your home, your church. I love coming here with you."

"Then I *do* have a little something to do with it?"

"You have everything to do with it," she said, and the love she saw in his eyes tore at her heart. It was so deep and sincere that for a moment she had to look away. Was she really sure she wanted Chris? For a lifetime? It would be so wrong if she were leading him on, even unintentionally.

"Will you marry me, Angel?" he said, holding her in a grip of steel. "I want to love and take care of you always. And I'll be good to you. I just pray to God I can make you happy." He bent and smothered her face with tender kisses.

"Chris, you're so good," she said in a few moments. "You've done so much for Cindy."

"Is that your answer to my proposal? Because if it is, I can't accept it. First of all, because it's God at work in Cindy's life, not me. Anyway, I don't want you to marry me out of any kind of gratitude."

"I wouldn't do that."

"Will you marry me for any reason?"

"I. . .I don't know yet."

"Diana, do I have to ask?"

She stared up at him, a quizzical look flickering in her eyes. "Ask what?"

"It seems to me the essential ingredient is missing here. On your part."

"I don't understand."

"If you marry me, I want you to marry me because you *love* me."

Impulsively she wrapped her slender arms around his neck, "I do love you, Chris. I do."

And she did, didn't she? Oh, if only she were sure!

He gave her a fiery kiss. And then, "Come on, I want to show you something," he said, his gentle voice bursting with joy and pride and contentment.

They walked hand in hand for some distance along the creek bank, past tall trees and meandering grass, until they reached a place where the land grew to a small rise. On the other side the creek dipped into a natural waterfall.

"This is where I'd like to build our house," Chris said, sliding an arm around her back. "There's something about the sound of water pouring over a waterfall." He smiled. "We could nestle our house over there not too far from the creek." He pointed to a spot just beyond where they stood. "Among those sycamore trees." He closed his arm around her waist and pulled her to him. "Would you like that, sweetheart?"

She gazed up at the love and happiness in his face. "I'd like that very much."

"Can you understand, Angel, that the sound of water rushing over the rocks and the glint of sunlight filtering through the trees are the things God gives us that no one can take away? Even a tragedy like Cindy's hasn't robbed her of the feel of a soft breeze or the warmth of the day. The smell of roses covered with dew in the early morning, the touch and shape of a leaf as it blossoms, these are the things that really make us rich. The tall grass and the blue sky. Can you understand my love for all this? For this, and music, and what folks call the simple things in life? Good friends, home cooking, and church on Sunday?"

"I think I understand it perfectly." And deep in her heart Diana knew she wanted to be a part of it, to be with Chris and share his ideals for the rest of her days.

Cindy was sitting on the back porch swing when Chris and Diana ambled arm in arm up the walkway. "I've never seen nothing like it," she said as they took a seat beside her.

"What's that?" Chris said.

"A farm! A garden! It's a miracle. Your daddy showed me a row of little green bushes in the garden. He let me feel them. And when he dug underneath one of them you know what he pulled out? Potatoes! Little potatoes growing right there in the ground."

Chris laughed. "Where did you think they grew?"

Cindy ignored his teasing. "He showed me beans growing up on poles and cabbage sitting right on top of the ground just waiting for somebody to come along and pick it up. And corn growing on tall stalks. And your tomatoes are so big! He let me pick some to take home. He gave us some other kinda beans too, bunch beans I think he called them. We picked them off little bushy plants on the ground."

"You think you'd like farming, Cinderella?"

"Yeah, I'd like it a lot."

"It's hard work," Chris said. "You can't get anything back from the land if you don't put something into it."

"Are you and Diana gonna live here when you get married?" Cindy asked, then blushed beet-red. "Oops, I guess I spoke out too soon."

Chris laughed. "I guess we'll have to build a pretty big house. We'll need a bedroom for us and one for you and a couple more to fill up later on."

"Oh, Chris!" Cindy cried. "You all *are* gonna get married and I'm gonna live with you?"

He laughed again. "What did you think we were going

to do, turn you out in the street?''

"No, but I don't think I should stay with you. You all should be by yourselves. I can live with Aunt Vi.''

"We want you with us," Chris said and glanced at Diana. She nodded.

"Are you sure?" asked Cindy.

"I don't want to hear anymore about it," Chris said. "It's all settled.''

• • •

Diana had just stepped into the living room when the telephone rang. She put down her purse on the coffee table and hurried to the hall to answer it.

"You just get home from work, Angel? I've been trying to call.''

"Yes, I only walked in this minute. Where are you?"

"Pledgerville.''

"When will you be home?"

"Hey, do I hear an I-miss-you sound in your voice?"

"I wish you were coming home tonight," she confessed.

"We won't be back till next week. I'm sorry I didn't call last night. I meant to during intermission, but some people came up and got to talking, and then we had to go back on. It was real late when we got off. The people kept asking to hear more songs. Well, I have to go now. I love you, Angel.''

"I love you.''

"I'll see you as soon as I get back.''

Diana was hanging up when Cindy came in the door. "Was that Chris?" she asked.

"Yes.''

"When will he be home?"

"Next week sometime.''

"Did he say what day?"

"No, why?"

"Do you think he'll sing at our revival next week? The choir director asked me if I thought he'd come.''

"You know he will if he gets back in time.''

Chapter Twenty-One _____

Aunt Vi trotted up the walk, a package tucked securely under her arm. As she neared the apartment house a cream-colored Celica pulled to a stop at the curb. The man behind the wheel climbed out and greeted her with a smile.

"Afternoon, Chris," said Aunt Vi. "Sure is nice to see you back! Isn't it hot today?"

"It's even hot out at the farm," he said, "No breeze at all."

"Will you be home for a while now?"

"For a few days. Then we're off again. July's a busy month for us."

At the apartment building Chris held open the front door for her. Inside the cool foyer he inquired of Cindy's whereabouts.

"She went upstairs a while ago as I was going over to the shopping center. She and Beth and Corey have been out most of the day giving out more handbills for the revival. Those girls are going to collapse if they're not careful. I told them it was too hot to be out today, but they wanted to go anyway."

Laughing, Chris said farewll to Aunt Vi and mounted the stairs. In the upstairs hallway he knocked at the first door on the left.

"Who is it?" called Cindy.

"How quickly they forget," he said mockingly. "You mean you didn't recognize my footsteps?"

Cindy flung the door wide open. "Chris! I was hoping

you'd get back today!''

He wrapped her in his arms for a bearlike hug. "Well, here I am, what's all the excitement?"

She went to the coffee table and picked up one of the handbills lying there. "This," she said, offering him a piece of white paper with bold black print. "Diana did them. Everybody says they're really good."

"They're great!" He laid the paper back down. "I saw Aunt Vi downstairs. She said you've been out with your friends giving these out."

"Did you read the part about the special music every night?"

"Yes."

"Well, I was wondering, that is, our choir director asked me if you might come and sing one night."

"What night did you have in mind?"

"You mean you will? Really? Without your group? Just you?"

"Well, I know I'm not much without the rest of the guys, but I'll give it a try if you want me to."

"Oh, I do! And the church will pay you—"

"Hey, I'm surprised at you, Cinderella. Don't you know me better than that? I'll enjoying singing at your church. I don't want to get paid for it. When does your choir director want me?"

"Tonight."

"You were cutting it kind of close, weren't you?" he laughed.

"Well, they don't have anything special planned tonight. If you didn't get back, the choir was going to sing. They've been rehearsing just in case."

"That would probably be better. Tell them to go ahead."

"Oh, you're teasing me. You will sing, won't you?"

"Do I have to?" he said, pretending a sorrowful tone.

She giggled. "Oh, stop. Does Diana know you're home?"

"No." He glanced at his watch. "She'll be getting off soon, won't she?"

"At five. She's been working more since she graduated, mostly during the day."

"Has she heard anymore from the public relations office at the seminary?"

"No. But she said she probably wouldn't hear anymore till September. That's when there's supposed to be an opening."

Cindy started for the kitchen. "While you go get Diana, I'm gonna start supper. The revival starts at seven." She paused in the middle of the floor. "Thanks, Chris."

"For what?"

"For...for a lot of things. For singing tonight. And... and...mostly helping me understand things better."

Diana had told him about Cindy's reconciliation with Mr. Denny, but Chris couldn't accept credit from her anymore than he had accepted it from her sister. "I suppose I have a pretty big mouth sometimes. Maybe somehow God can use that. But, honey, don't ever get confused about who really brings about the good in our lives. Every good thing comes from Him."

"There's more good, Chris," Cindy said. "The McIntoshes have been going to church with us ever since they heard your group at the auditorium. They like the way you all presented the gospel so much they wanted to find out more about it."

Chris grinned joyfully. "You don't know how good that makes me feel. That's why we like to sing, to help people find Jesus. And then bring them closer to Him."

At the revival later that evening, Cindy told Diana what Chris had said. Listening to his expressive version of "Without Him," Diana couldn't imagine hearing the Good News presented any more beautifully than when Chris sang of it.

How could anyone do without a Lord who gave His people such wonderful blessings? The loss of Cindy's sight had been almost more than the young girl could cope with, but she still had the precious gift of hearing. Whatever would her sister do, Diana wondered, if she couldn't hear Chris sing about Jesus anymore?

● ● ●

Diana and Cindy were in the kitchen making supper. The smell of biscuits wafted up from the oven as Cindy carried a bowl of fried potatoes to the table. "I thought all this rain would cool things off," she said.

"Hasn't yet," Diana commented, setting a plate of sausage patties next to the range for Cindy to take to the table. Her sister brought coleslaw from the refrigerator and placed that along with the sausages on the table.

"Will Chris be back tonight?" she asked.

"I don't think so. He didn't say anything about it when he called last night."

"He's called you almost every night. Boy, he sure must love you a lot."

"As soon as the biscuits come out," Diana said, bending over the oven, "we can eat."

Footsteps on the stairs in the hallway sent Cindy to the living room. "That must be Mr. Denny. He said he'd come over and eat with us tonight. Only that doesn't sound like his knock."

At the door Cindy opened it wide and Chris strode into the room with his easy, carefree bounce. He carried a large bag under his arm. "It's really coming down out there." He gave Cindy a peck on the cheek as he headed for the kitchen.

"What are you doing here?" the girl said.

"I came to see you, what else?" To Diana he added, "I brought you some fresh vegetables from the farm."

She turned from the oven with the pan of biscuits as Chris set down the sack of vegetables on the counter. "Why didn't you tell me last night that you'd be home tonight?"

"I thought I'd surprise you. Aren't you glad to see me?"

Diana placed the biscuits in a basket on the table and returned the pan to the range. Then she came to him and slipped her arms up around his neck. "What do you think?"

"I'm wet," he said.

"I don't care."

He gazed down into her eyes for a lingering moment. "No, I don't believe you do." He took her in his arms then for a thorough, intimate kiss. "It sure is good to be here with you. Talking over the phone isn't enough."

Cindy layed another place setting at the table and Mr. Denny arrived as she was admonishing the "lovebirds" to sit down to supper before everything got cold. After Chris offered the blessing and the food was being passed, he talked with the handyman about various topics until Cindy spoke up.

"You sure timed it right, Chris, getting here just when Diana got supper ready. Diana's a great cook. You'll like that after you all get married. What's your favorite food?"

"I like anything, Cinderella. I don't think I'm too hard to please."

"But you must like something special."

"You know what I really like? Peanut butter. Peanut butter and banana sandwiches. Fried."

"Are you kidding me?"

"No, I'm not. I ate a lot of those when I was a kid. When you come from poor beginnings you learn to like what you have."

"I guess Diana can make peanut butter and banana sandwiches all right. But fried?"

Everyone laughed and Chris said, "Mom used to fix them that way so they'd taste a little different."

"When do you have to leave again, Chris?" Diana said then.

"Day after tomorrow. We'll be gone a couple weeks." He furrowed his brow. "I don't like the way I've been feeling lately. I love singing, but I want to be with you, too. We're going to have to work something out soon. You being in one place and me in another isn't doing me any good."

"When you and Diana get married, you'll still be gone a lot," Cindy said.

"She can go with me then, Cinderella. At least till we decide to start a family, and then we wouldn't be separated too much, except in the summer."

"Maybe I won't take that job at the seminary," Diana said.

Chris looked surprised. "Of course you'll take the job, if you want it. It won't be far to drive from the farm. We're in a good location, close to town and the interstate, but away from the crowded city life."

"Maybe I'll only work part-time at the seminary. I can work

at home too, for Marshall's and other places. I want to be with you, Chris. I want to travel with you for awhile."

"Cinderella, you can travel with us too during the summer," the singer said, "and on weekends when you're not in school."

"I'd really like that."

"You both need the experience of traveling to complete your educations. We might try to go to Europe next year." Chris winked across the table at Mr. Denny. Then he reached out and put an arm around each of the girls. "Whether we're traveling or at home, we'll make a great little family, the three of us."

•   •   •

When Chris and his group returned from a round of concerts two weeks later, he couldn't wait to pick up Diana and take her out to the farm. Cindy had gone to a swim party with her youth group that Saturday afternoon, and so after the evening meal it was just the two of them in the swing on the back porch. Mr. and Mrs. Jarrett had convincingly excused themselves to the living room to watch a popular program on television.

"I think this is my favorite time of day," he said, slipping an arm around her shoulders and gazing off into a western sky splashed with crimson, gold, and azure, "when the sun is going down and the day cools off. Soon the crickets will start chirping and there will be a breeze. Do you really like it out here, Angel?"

"Very much."

"You don't mind that we come here a lot when I'm home?"

She looked over at him. "No, why should I?"

"I mean instead of going out somewhere to eat."

"Oh, no, Chris. You have to eat out all the time when you're on the road. I know how much it must mean to you to come home and have a home-cooked meal."

"It will mean even more to me when we have our own house. I plan to start on it this fall. We'll stay at your apartment, I guess, till we get it built." Suddenly he turned to her. "You know, I'm not against you, or any woman, working, not basically. But I guess being a Southern gentleman—I hope I am—I've got old-fashioned ideas about what God intended woman's role to be. I believe men are meant to be the buffers for women in the world, and that a woman makes a warm, loving atmosphere for man to come home to after the day's battles. A place where he can keep his sanity."

"I think a lot of women who are so career-oriented might be that way because they aren't appreciated at home. If husbands loved their wives the way God intended, I don't see how they could be dissatisfied."

"Satan is destroying this country through the breakdown of the home. I don't want that to happen to us. We'll have to work at making our home what God wants it to be."

"Chris, my career will always be important to me. I have some talent, I should use it. But my children and husband will come first, after the Lord. What could come before shaping the character of another human being? Through being a mother, of sorts, to Cindy, I've learned that a child is the most precious gift God can bestow."

Chris smiled tenderly at her. In a minute he ran his fingers lightly over the hair falling in soft chestnut waves down her back. "Have I ever told you how much I like your hair?"

"No."

"It's beautiful. Will you do something for me? Don't ever cut it off."

"All right, Chris."

"I love to look at it and feel it. It feels like silk." His heart swelled with emotion and he closed her in a powerful embrace, seeking her lips passionately, forcefully beneath his own. "My angel," he whispered later into the softness of her hair. "I love you so much. I sure don't want to leave you again. But this will be the last time. I promise."

"The last time?"

"We'll be gone three weeks. After that you're going with me. I'm getting tired of kissing you good-bye all the time. I'm going to do something about that as soon as we get back."

Diana sat up. "What are you going to do?"

He laughed softly. "We're going to put all this talk into action. We're going to get married." As an afterthought, he said, "You know something? I haven't even bought you an engagement ring."

"Chris, I know we've been talking about getting married, but I didn't think it would be so soon."

"What do you mean, 'so soon'? I feel like I've waited an eternity for you."

She studied him in the dying evening light. He wore such a sweet, sincere expression. And she really did love him. So why did she want to wait to marry him?

"I don't think we should rush."

"We aren't rushing, Angel. But I want you with me. I want to take care of you."

"I know, but...I just want to wait."

"No. It's all settled. You've got three weeks to pick out your dress and trousseau. The quartet's got a couple weeks off the first of September. Where would you like to go on our honeymoon?"

"Please, Chris, won't you listen?"

"Nothing you can say will change my mind."

"I want to wait a little longer. Maybe when the quartet takes some time off for Christmas."

"There's no reason to wait till then."

"But—"

"We're getting married when I get back."

"No!"

He turned, taking her by the shoulders and staring at the unrest in her eyes. "What do you mean, 'no'?"

"I don't want to get married...not yet."

"Why not?"

"I...I just...can't."

He let go of her. "You still don't trust me completely, do you?"

"Yes I do. Love and trust go together, don't they?"

"I've always thought they did."

"Please try to understand, Chris, please. I was hurt

once...terribly. And I—"

"I know. Cindy told me about it." Shortly he said. "I've never asked you this, but are you still in love with the guy you were engaged to?"

"No. I realized a long time ago that marrying him would have been a mistake. It was really a blessing that he broke it off."

"Then you're just afraid. But you don't have to fear me. You're worth everything to me. You're all I think about, you're all I want for my whole life. I will *never* hurt you like that."

The devotion flowing from his beautiful eyes made her want to believe him. She felt almost as if she could. Almost.

"Can't we wait a while? Give me just a little more time."

He shook his head. "When the quartet gets back we're getting married. If you want to marry me. If you don't..."

Chapter Twenty-Two _____

The Jarretts left for their final summer tour two days later, and Diana was left with the biggest decision of her young life. She spent all of her prayer and devotion time each morning asking God to guide her in the choice she made. Her talks with Him at the end of the day were filled with this request. But even while she studied and communed with the Lord, she knew she could never give Chris up. Her love for the singer was confirmed in every breath she drew, it seemed, and still in that she couldn't manage to offer him the whole of her heart, at peace and free of any doubt from the past.

One morning when Diana sat at the kitchen table reading her Bible, she found herself in the Book of Psalms going over some of the many references there about trusting God to guide a Christian in all things. In Psalm 2:12, she read that "Blessed are they that put their trust in Him." In Psalm 71:5, she found, "For thou art my hope, O Lord God: thou art my trust from my youth."

Yes, she trusted God completely. But had she put her total faith in Him this way when she had said yes to Glen two years ago? She couldn't remember doing so. Had that been why she had made such an unwise decision back then? Had God shown His perfect love for her by allowing her to suffer the hurt of a broken engagement so that her trust in Him could be strengthened? So that she would let Him guide her to the person He chose, knowing this man would be the right one?

From Proverbs 3 this Scripture came to her mind: "In all thy ways acknowlege Him and He shall direct thy paths."

God's Word had taught Diana to trust Him in everything and He would lead her in every way. That included the choice of a husband. And as she put that choice completely in God's care that morning, her fingers seemed to fly through the Bible to 2 Timothy 1:7. She read aloud the words: "For God hath not given us the spirit of fear; but of power, and of love, and of a sound mind."

And then Diana knew. Fear had been tricking her. But God in His wisdom had given her Chris to love and trust completely through Him. An exquisite peace settled over her then and when she finally closed her Bible and prepared to leave for work, she was no longer bothered by doubts. A never-ending joy had replaced her fears and she began counting the days and hours until Chris' return.

• • •

Cindy and Beth trod the walkway to the apartment house. "Do you think Diana might want to go down to the community center with us?" Beth was saying.

"I doubt it," Cindy replied. "She's awful busy making plans these days. She and Chris are going to set the date for their wedding when he gets back tomorrow night. But he doesn't know it yet. She hasn't told Chris when he's called that she's ready to get married. She wants to surprise him."

"I thought Diana had an extra-special look about her these days."

"Wouldn't you look special, Beth, if you were gonna marry Chris Jarrett? He's just the best person in the whole world."

Diana was rummaging in the back of the closet in her bedroom when she heard the girls come in. In a minute they appeared in the bedroom doorway.

"Diana we're gonna walk down to the community center," Cindy said. "They're having a talent show tonight and an arts and crafts exhibit. And a lot of neat things."

"Don't you want some supper before you go?" Diana asked,

turning from the closet with several dresses on her arm.

"No, we'll get a Coke and hot dog at the center."

"You need some money?"

"No, I have some. We won't be out late."

"You want to come with us?" Beth interjected.

"No, thanks, Beth," said Diana. "I'm knee-deep in going through some old clothes I don't wear anymore. I have quite a few things I want to get ready for the clothes closet for the needy at church."

"What's she's really doing," Cindy said, "is cleaning out her closet to make room for Chris' clothes. They're gonna live here for a while after they get married, till they get their house built out on his farm."

Beth and Cindy had gone and Diana was looking over a pant suit in a style popular several years ago, when the buzzer sounded at the door. She tossed the suit on the bed and went to answer it.

"Hi, Diana."

"Hello, Walt."

"May I come in?"

"Well, I . . ."

He glanced around the living room. "Oh, you busy?"

Walt Ames was a heavyset, nice-looking young man with dark hair and eyes. He was a nephew of Mrs. McIntosh and had come to Briarton a week before to enroll in classes at the seminary. He had been staying with the McIntoshes until he could get a room on campus. To Diana he had become, quite frankly, a bit of a pest. She had made it plain to him that she was committed elsewhere, and he often talked about a girl friend in his hometown in another state, but she assumed he was lonely away from everything and everyone familiar. And so, she had been pleasant, even friendly, to him and had introduced him to others their age at church. But Walt hadn't seemed to take up with anyone else. He made it clear in the past few days that he preferred Diana's company.

"I'm not really busy, Walt," she said, not wanting to be rude. He stepped into the room before he had actually been invited and with a weary sigh Diana closed the door behind him. She motioned him to a seat. "Will you have a glass of tea?"

"Yes, thanks." He sat down on the loveseat and watched her in the kitchen filling two glasses from an amber pitcher. Back in the living room she gave him one of the long glasses and then took a seat across from him in the chair beside the stereo. "So what are you doing tonight?" he asked before taking a drink from his glass.

"Actually, I was cleaning out my closet when you came."

"Sounds like a dull evening."

Diana sipped her tea and smiled at him. "Not really." *Not when you're cleaning it out to share with your future husband.*

"Have you eaten?" Walt said in a minute.

"No."

"What do you say we go out and get something?" She was about to protest when he went on, "I know. You said you're going with someone. And I'm not trying to beat his time. Honestly I'm not. But if he's out of town like you said, can't we go somewhere as two friends? Nothing more, I promise."

"I'm sorry, Walt. I really can't. I know you don't mean it as anything other than a gesture of friendship, but I don't want to go anywhere tonight."

"What's the matter, doesn't your boyfriend trust you?"

"Of course he does!" Diana flared, feeling a dislike for this fellow all of a sudden. "Chris trusts me completely. As I trust him." *Now,* she thought. *And with God's precious guidance.*

"Chris who?" Walt asked skeptically.

"Chris Jarrett."

"Chris Jarrett? The famous gospel singer? He's your boyfriend? I don't think you mentioned that before."

"He's more than just my boyfriend," she said, "We're engaged. When he gets back tomorrow we're going to set the date for our wedding."

Walt set his glass of iced tea in a silver coaster on the coffee table as he glanced at Diana's left hand. "You aren't wearing a ring." He regarded her speculatively for a moment. "Are you sure you're not making this whole thing up?"

"I'm not making it up. Chris has been so busy this summer we just haven't had time to pick out a ring."

"Convenient."

With mounting irritation Diana rose and placed her glass beside Walt's. "I think you'd better go now," she said. "I have a lot of work I need to get done tonight."

He came to his feet and strode to her side. "All right, Diana, I'll go if that's the way you want it. But you can tell me the truth. You don't have to invent a story to get rid of me."

"I didn't invent anything. I'm telling you the truth. I'm engaged to Chris Jarrett."

He smiled slowly. "If that's the way you want it."

At the door Walt stepped out in the hall and Diana bade him good night. She was about to close the door when he leaned over, one hand resting on each side of the doorjamb. "One little kiss between friends before I go? Just to show there's no hard feelings?"

Diana only had time to look horrified before she heard the front door open in the foyer downstairs and someone mount the steps. Then Walt bent and kissed her mouth. She drew back at once and Walt turned around, a look of speechless amazement coming over his face. Diana glanced past him to Chris standing at the top of the steps staring at them in utter disbelief.

"Hello, Angel," he said in a minute. "We got back a day early and I couldn't wait to see you."

The past came down on Chris then, swelling, hurtling like an avalanche gone out of control. It had happened like this once before. He had just walked in and caught them together. No forewarning. Not even the slightest indication. But Diana would never do such a thing. She couldn't. Oh, she had been undecided about marrying him three weeks ago, but still she wouldn't do a thing like this to him. Would she?

She surely had a look of love about her tonight he had not seen before. Where did she get this happy sparkle all of a sudden? She had always been a shining, vital person—that was one of the qualities he loved most about her—that was what had attracted him to her in the beginning. But this look was something new. Had her old flame come back? Had she decided to marry him after all?

Chris stood there a moment longer, staring in shock, before he started back down the steps.

Diana went after him. "Chris! Wait! Please!"

At the front door he stopped and whirled around. Bewilderment and pain and disgrace met her gaze. He wanted to tell her how it felt to go through all this again. He wanted to explain the shock, the hurt, the humiliation. But he couldn't. He could only look at her and hurt. Not Diana, his heart cried. Not his angel. She couldn't do this. Slowly, very slowly his anger began to rise.

"Please wait!" she was imploring from the stairs.

His jaw throbbed achingly and his teeth clenched tightly together. "Chris has waited as long as he's going to."

"But I can explain!"

He shook his head.

"Yes, Chris, please!"

He turned back to the door as she called out to him, desperation in her voice, "Chris, don't go! If you love me you'll listen!"

He paused, still stunned, reaching for the doorknob. Without looking up, he said, "I guess I don't love you."

He gave the doorknob a violent jerk and in a flash he was outside and gone. The slamming of the door echoed in Diana's ears like an erupting volcano.

*Chapter Twenty-Three*_____

It wasn't late when Cindy returned. But hearing no sounds in the apartment, she called out from inside the door. "Diana, you still up?"

"I'm here," in a voice barely above a whisper.

Cindy faced the couch. Ever-sensitive to Diana's tone, she said, "What's wrong? Are you sick?"

"No."

Cindy made her way across the room and took a place beside her sister. "What is it?"

"I don't know how to explain it. It's all so crazy."

"What is?"

"Chris. What happened. Everything."

Cindy went tense. "Has something happened to Chris? Did they have an accident?"

Diana said, from an almost trance-like state, "He said he doesn't love me."

"What do you mean? That's crazy."

"He came here tonight. They got back early. Walt was here and . . ."

After Diana told her sister what took place while she had been at the community center, the girl was strangely silent for a time. Finally, she said, "What did Walt do after Chris left?"

"He felt awful. He wanted to go after Chris and explain. But I wouldn't let him. Chris was so angry he wouldn't listen to anybody. He wouldn't even let me explain who Walt was and

175

how that horrible kiss came about.''

"Diana, I think I know why. He was hurt once before just like you were. Only it was even worse, I guess. The girl broke off with him just three weeks before the wedding. She ran off with some rich guy from Canada. Marlene told me about it.''

"Then Chris must have thought...oh, Cindy, he thought I...''

It was all her own fault, Diana silently chided. She had been so unsure about marrying Chris. And then when he had come here tonight to get her final answer, he found another man kissing her. No wonder he assumed the worst. Now that she understood why, could she blame him? If only she had told him over the phone that she was ready to set the date for the wedding. If only she hadn't wanted to surprise him. Instead the surprise had been hers. And what hurt most of all was that he had said he didn't love her.

"Maybe he just said it 'cause he was hurt," Cindy said when Diana shared this most painful thought. "Chris loves you, Diana. I know that as well as I know my own name.''

"And I love him. Completely. But it's too late now.''

"Maybe not," Cindy said in an effort to cheer her sister. "Give him time to cool off. Then he'll listen to you.''

"And just listen to you," said Diana, "giving your big sister advice. Things sure have changed around here.''

In spite of the ray of hope Cindy's words had given Diana, nothing seemed changed in regard to her relationship with Chris. She waited three days and when he didn't call or come by she telephoned out to the farm. His mother was kind to her, but could only relate her son's message, that if Diana tried to get in touch with him, he didn't want to talk to her. She was tempted to pour out the whole story in Mrs. Jarrett's sympathetic ear, wondering what, if anything, Chris had told her. She was certain the older woman would understand the situation and tell her son he was making a grave misjudgment. But pride kept her from breaking down; and she decided that, after all, if Chris' mother did believe her explanation, it was almost a certainty that her son would not, that he would think she was using his mother's soft heart to get to him.

The Saturday night gospel sing came two weeks after Chris and Diana's fateful parting. Craig Jarvis asked Diana if he could walk down to the auditorium with Cindy; and after giving her consent, especially since Beth and Corey would also be going with them, she gave thoughtful consideration to whether or not she would go, too. It was tempting to try to see Chris at intermission or after the concert. Perhaps by this time he would be willing to listen to reason. But if not it would be wrong to maybe upset him while he was performing or meeting people, and how humiliating it would be if he refused to talk to her. And she couldn't bear to see him look so pained and hear him say again, *"I guess I don't love you."*

• • •

The concert had just started and as Cindy and her friends were seated, the quartet's lead singer was beginning a powerful solo. His voice seemed greater than ever, but Cindy could hear the agony in his tone as he sang. He sounded like a man tormented.

Once I stood in the night with my head bowed low,
In the darkness as black as could be;
And my heart felt alone, And I cried,
"O Lord, don't hide your face from me."

Like a king I may live in a palace so tall
With great riches to call my own;
But I don't know a thing in this whole wide world
That's worse than being alone.

The rest of the quartet joined Chris on the chorus, but Cindy could clearly discern the tremendous range of his baritone as he reached so expertly for the notes:

Hold my hand all the way, ev'ry hour, ev'ry day,
From here to the great unknown.
Take my hand, let me stand Where no one stands alone.
Take my hand, let me stand Where no one stands alone.

At intermission the auditorium flooded with light and everywhere people got up and started for the doors leading to the lobby. Cindy left Craig waiting for her by the refreshment stand as she carefully made her way to the table where The Jarretts sold their records. Diana would be furious if she knew what Cindy was up to. But she felt it was worth a try. She had to. Chris and Diana loved each other and it would be worth anything to get them back together. If she only could!

She had no elaborate plan. Just the simple truth. Aunt Vi had always said that worked best. And occasionally if it didn't, at least you felt good for having spoken it. And so, she would tell Chris who Walt Ames was and why he had been with Diana that night. She would tell him about Diana's surprise, her readiness to set the date for their wedding. Or maybe she would save that for Diana to tell. It would depend on Chris. And anyway, her sister would be angry enough that she had even talked to him, that she had broken another promise, for that had been the only way Diana would consent to her coming to the concert. If she gave her word not to talk to Chris about what happened.

At the table where The Jarretts sold their records Cindy listened intently above the din of conversation for Chris' soft drawl. She heard the deep tone of the group's bass singer and the sound of the second tenor. Finally she recognized a third voice and made her way toward it.

"Cindy!" said Billy. "How've you been, honey? Haven't seen you for a while."

"I'm just fine. How's Marlene and little Mike?"

"They're fine. You ought to see that little rascal now. You wouldn't know him. He's getting so big. He eats more than I do now."

"Oh, sure he does," Cindy laughed. Then, "Billy, Chris isn't out here, is he?"

"No. He's back in the dressing room."

"Do you think I could go back and talk to him?"

"Well, sure you can." He paused to say something to the man standing next to him. "Come on, I'll take you back there now."

Backstage, Billy guided the girl down a long, narrow hallway. At the end he came to a stop at a door on the left. "Do you want me to go in with you?"

"No. I'd sorta like to talk to Chris by myself."

"Sure thing. See you later, honey."

"So long, Billy. And thanks."

As Billy's footsteps echoed down the corridor, Cindy knocked softly at the door. When Chris called for her to come in, she turned the knob and stepped noiselessly inside, closing the door quietly behind her. Chris sat in a chair facing a small dressing table. He had removed his suit coat and sat slumped forward with his head resting in his hands. Cindy couldn't see him, but she sensed the melancholy that surrounded his presence.

She wanted to say so many things all of a sudden. She longed to let him know that she understood how he felt, that she hurt too, that he wasn't alone in his sorrow. It was because of his hurting and sorrow that she knew beyond a doubt how much he loved Diana. Only someone who had so loved could be so in pain. But she scarcely knew how to convey all she felt. How inadequate mere words could be sometimes!

"Hi, Chris."

He looked around then and came to his feet. "Hello, Cinderella."

"I...I hope I'm not bothering you."

He pushed back the chair and came across the floor. "No, of course not. How are you, honey?"

"I'm fine." Then, haltingly, "How've you been, Chris?"

"I'm doing fine."

"I wasn't sure if I should come or not."

"Why shouldn't you come? You come to see me any time you want. And so, how's everybody? Aunt Vi and Mr. Denny?"

"They're fine. Mr. Denny's feeling lots better now. He can do almost everything he did before."

"That's good news. How's school this year?"

"I've got some new teachers, I really like them." After a pause, she said, "Do you want to know about Craig?"

"Oh, yeah. Good ol' Craig. The handsome prince."

Cindy smiled shyly. "He's waiting for me out in the lobby. He's so nice to me, Chris. We go for walks and he describes everything to me. I remember a lot of things, but he tells me when something is different now."

"Is this turning into a serious romance, little lady?"

"Oh, you're teasing me."

"You know I wouldn't do that. But some day you'll settle on a young man and I sure don't envy him."

"You don't?"

"He'll have a mighty hard time getting past Chris Jarrett's inspection."

"Oh, Chris."

"I mean it. It'll take a special person for you, Cinderella. A *real* prince."

Into the awkward silence that came between them, Cindy finally said, "I've sure been missing you."

"I've missed you, too."

"Ain't you never coming back to see us?"

"I'm sorry, sweetheart, but I guess not."

"But Diana wants you to. She—"

"Did she send you down here to tell me that?" he broke in.

"Oh, no! She made me promise I wouldn't talk to you. But...I guess I sorta broke my promise. Again."

"You didn't need to do that."

"Yes, I did. Oh, Chris, you don't understand. It's not what you think at all. You see, Walt's just a friend. He's Mrs. McIntosh's nephew who's come here to the seminary. He and Diana had just met the week before you got back and she'd told him all about you. He just came to see her right before you got there. But she really doesn't like him very much. She's only nice to him so she won't hurt his feelings. But he likes her, I guess, and he had to go and kiss her. Diana didn't know he was gonna do that. She was as shocked as you were."

When the singer offered no comment to Cindy's explanation, she said, "Don't you believe me, Chris?"

"No, I don't believe you."

She felt hot tears prick her eyelids. "But you've got to! It's true! It is! I wouldn't lie to you, don't you know that?''

"For Diana you might. But I admit I'm surprised she's used you this way. Maybe after her last surprise, though, I shouldn't wonder at anything she does."

"Chris! You don't sound like yourself. You sound bitter like I used to."

"I'm not bitter, just..."

"You're hurt like Diana," she said when he didn't go on. "She's so hurt she cries every night. I guess I shouldn't tell you that. But I can hear her after I go to bed. She thinks I'm asleep, but I hear her in her room, crying and crying. I guess that's what really made me come here tonight. I had to try to do something to stop her tears."

"Stop it!" Chris stormed. "It won't work, Cindy!"

"But I'm telling you the truth! What's the matter with you? You talked to me about love and trust. But where's yours? You used to love Diana. Even though she's hurt you so much—you think—you couldn't have stopped loving her already. It has to take a long time for that to go away."

"A man can learn to forget mighty quick. All it takes is practice."

"Oh, Chris, she was gonna surprise you. I'm not supposed to tell you, but she realized while you were gone that she loved and trusted you with all her heart. She was planning on you all setting the date for the wedding when you got back. She—"

A knock sounded at the door then and Billy thrust his head into the room. "Ready, Chris?"

The singer nodded and turned to the dressing table to get his suit coat draped over the back of the chair. Billy disappeared as Chris came over to Cindy. "I'm sorry, Cinderella, but we have to go back on stage now."

"Please, Chris, don't you believe what I've told you? Diana really loves you and wants to marry you."

"There's only so much a man can take, honey."

"I know. You got hurt before too. But—"

"How do you know about that?"

"Marlene told me. But this isn't like that."

"Diana doesn't love me or trust me. I've known that all along. I just didn't want to believe it."

"No! I told you—"

"I have to go now, honey. You coming?"

The girl stood her ground, only her mouth trembled to give away her pain and anger. "One time you told me God's love was tough. You said a Christian has to have tough love, too. What's happened to your tough love, Chris? *What's happened to it?*"

In the absence of any response, Cindy at last said, "You told me something else, too. You told me Helen Keller said the greatest tragedy in the world was to have eyes and not be able to see. Not be able to see the truth and what really matters. What's wrong with your eyes, Chris? Can't you see anymore either?"

He stared down at her, with an expression Cindy couldn't see. It seemed like an eternity before he turned and without a word strode out the door and down the hallway.

Chapter Twenty-Four _____

Cindy was on the front porch helping Mr. Denny polish the leaves of the great emerald philodendrons flanking each side of the front door.

"I remember everything you told me about taking care of plants," she was saying. "I hope when I have a house of my own I can have lots of them. Do you think I'll be able to take care of them by myself?"

"You'll take care of them just the way I've taught you," said Mr. Denny. "Just remember my motto—do as little as possible."

"I remember—keep the leaves clean and water them only when they need it. Put your finger in the soil and see if they're dry. And when you replant, do it only in the next largest size pot."

"I think you've got it, Cindy," the handyman said as he straightened from the plant he had been cleaning.

"Come and see if I've got all the dust off these leaves," she requested.

He gave the philodendron a close examination. "You're doing a fine job. I may promote you to my assistant after this."

"I thought I *was* your assistant," she said, looking briefly puzzled.

"So you are," the old man chuckled. He glanced up as a cream-colored Celica pulled up before the walkway.

The tall, broad-shouldered man behind the wheel climbed out

and started toward them, smiling in the afternoon sunlight.

Cindy said, "Who's coming, Mr. Denny?" But before the handyman could answer she cried, "It's Chris! It's Chris! I'd know his walk anywhere!"

The singer had no sooner stepped up on the porch than Cindy hurled herself squarely into his arms. He laughed and whirled her round and round.

"You must have on a whole bottle of after-shave lotion," she said, "but I still don't think you're a brute."

Laughing some more, Chris greeted Mr. Denny, shaking hands with the older man and inquiring about his health.

"What are you doing here?" Cindy wanted to know at once. "Have you come to see Diana?" she said, her face suddenly aglow with delight.

"Is she home now?"

"Boy, I'll say. She's home all the time these days."

Chris glanced from the girl to Mr. Denny. "What are you talking about?"

"Diana fell and broke her ankle the other day," Cindy informed him. "She fell down the steps just like Mr. Denny did. Aunt Vi says those steps are a jinx now and maybe she ought to put in an elevator."

Chris was already past Cindy, opening the front door. "I'll see you later," he said over his shoulder. "Why didn't you let me know about this?"

"Just go on in, Chris," the girl called as he disappeared inside. "The door isn't locked."

Diana was propped up on the couch with pillows behind her head and a pillow under her left leg. She was wrapped in a thick white cast from the toes of her left foot up to her knee. She had on a pink robe and her hair was brushed into soft curls around her shoulders.

When Diana glanced up and saw him striding confidently into the room, a light suddenly came on in her heart. Perhaps it was how handsome he looked in gray slacks and shirt, perhaps it was the look on his face that told her more than any words could say; but for whatever reason, by the time he came across the floor to her side she was already crying, tears rolling in great drops onto her cheeks.

He knelt beside her on the carpet and gathered her into the quiet strength of his embrace.

"Oh, Chris, I'm so sorry," she sobbed. "I'm so sorry."

"Sorry for what? I'm the one who acted like a fool. You didn't do anything. I know that now."

"Oh, but I did. All the time I put you off, when really I loved you almost from the start."

"It's all right, Angel. That's all behind us."

"But I had so many doubts. If I hadn't felt like that, you probably wouldn't have thought Walt and I—"

"Let's not talk about that. Cindy explained all that to me."

Diana drew back. "She did? That girl sure doesn't know anything about keeping a promise."

"Thank God," he laughed.

"Oh, Chris, I've been such an imbecile. Darling, I love you so much. I never knew I could love anyone this much."

Chris, smiling at her, said, "I think I'm in the proper position for this." He reached into the pocket of his slacks then and pulled out a tiny velvet box. Inside he took a diamond solitaire ring from its satin resting place and slipped it on the third finger of her left hand. All Diana could do was gaze at him through thick, wet lashes until she broke into tears again.

He enfolded her in his powerful arms and bent to stop her crying with a kiss. With the salty taste of her tears on his lips, he said, "I love you forever, Diana, my angel, and if you'll have me back I'll spend my life trying to make you happy."

"Oh, Chris, " she moaned and tears poured once more from her eyes.

"What's the matter now, sweetheart? If all I do is make you cry maybe I'd better go."

She managed to stop crying long enough to look down at her cast. "I can't marry you like this! That's why I'm crying."

'Why can't you?"

"Some bride I'll make, hobbling down the aisle on crutches."

186 / THE TENDER MELODY

"What difference does that make? But if you'd rather, I'll carry you. Or we can wait till you get the cast off."

"But that's six whole weeks!"

"What's six weeks? I feel like I've been waiting for you a lifetime." He took a handkerchief from his back pocket then and said, "Can I get off my knees now? It's getting a little uncomfortable."

She laughed as he sank down on the rug and began wiping at her damp cheeks. "Thank you," she said in a minute. She studied her engagement ring. "I've never seen anything so beautiful."

"I have," he said, gazing into her eyes.

She flicked her glance up and met his vivid blue gaze. "Chris, is that why you came back, because of what Cindy told you?"

"Partly. She got me to thinking rationally again. After I thought about it, I knew she'd never lie to me, not even for you. She and I have something very special. But I came back for only one reason. I love you and want you to be my wife."

"I only want that to be a lifetime job." Impulsively she said, "Tell me about the house we're going to build."

"We'll build it any way you want."

"I want a fireplace."

When she didn't elaborate, he said, "Is that all? Don't you want a house to go with it?"

She laughed at him. "Sure, but as long as it's got a big fireplace, we can build around that."

"How many kids do you want? I think we ought to have a whole football team, don't you?"

"But that's eleven!" she admonished. "Nobody has eleven kids anymore."

"We'll start the old trend over. Eleven will do for a start."

"No, I don't think we should. There's too many people in the world to feed already. Let's just have six."

"Oh, a small family, only six, huh?"

"People still raise big families in the country, don't they?"

"Some do. Some raise big families in the city."

"Do you want boys or girls?"

"Three of each."

"We can try, but we'll have to take what we get."

"I'll be happy too."

"We can tell them scary stories around the fireplace on cold nights."

"While we're eating popcorn popped over the fire."

She reached out and touched his cheek, stroking it tenderly, lovingly. "We'll have to have a dog for all those kids. And maybe a cat. Cindy will like that, too." After a pause, she said, "Chris, will you do something for me?"

"Anything."

"You may think I'm being silly, but...do you know any songs besides hymns and gospel songs."

"Sure."

"Would you sing something to me now? A soft and tender melody. Sing a love song."

Chris smiled sweetly. "A song for an angel," he said and in a minute his golden voice was flowing gently in her ears:

You are My Special Angel Sent from up above,
The Lord smiled down on me and sent an angel to love,
You are My Special Angel Right from paradise,
I know that you're an angel Heaven's in your eyes.

A smile from your lips brings the summer sunshine,
The tears from your eyes bring the rain.
I feel your touch, your warm embrace,
And I'm in heaven again.

You are My Special Angel Through eternity,
I'll have My Special Angel here to watch over me.

The door opened then and Cindy came inside. "Diana, I brought you something," she said. "Mr. Denny and I went over to the shopping center and got it. It's for your trousseau. You'll be needing that now, won't you?" She crossed the room with a large bag in her hand.

"I can't wait to see what you got," Diana said, "but first I have something to show you."

She touched the ring on her finger and smiled lovingly at Chris.

ACKNOWLEDGMENTS

(Songs listed in order of appearance in story)

"My Singing Is A Prayer"
Words: Novella D. Preston, 1964.
Tune: VERMONT, David H. Williams, 1964
© Copyright 1964 Broadman Press
All rights reserved. Used by permission.

"In My Father's House Are Many Mansions" by Aileene Hanks.
© Copyright Jimmy Davis Music Co., Inc.
Renewed. All rights reserved. Used by permission.

"He Touched Me" by William J. Gaither.
© 1963 by William J. Gaither.
All rights reserved. Used by permission of Gaither Music Company.

"Happy Birthday To You" by Mildred J. Hill and Patty S. Hill.
© Copyright 1935 Summy-Birchard Music division of Birch Tree Group
Ltd. Copyright renewed. All rights reserved. Used by permission.

"If We Never Meet Again" by Albert E. Brumley.
© Copyright 1945 by Stamps Quartet Music Company in Divine Praises.
Assigned 1949 Stamps Quartet Music Company and Albert E. Brumley.
Renewal. All rights reserved. Used by permission.

"His Hand In Mine" by Mosie Lister and Don Becker.
© 1953 (Renewed) Warner Brothers Music Inc.
All rights reserved. Used by permission.

"Who Am I?" by Rusty Goodman.
© Copyright 1965 by First Monday Music (A Division of Word, Inc.)
All rights reserved. International copyright secured. Used by permission.

"How Great Thou Art" by Stuart K. Hine.
© Copyright 1953. Renewed 1981 by Manna Music, Inc., 2111 Kenmere
Ave., Burbank, CA 91504. International copyright secured.
All rights reserved. Used by permission.

"Where No One Stands Alone" by Mosie Lister.
© Copyright 1955. Renewed 1983 by Lillenas Publishing Co.
All rights reserved. Used by permission.

"My Special Angel" by Jimmy Duncan.
© Copyright 1957 Warner-Tamerlane Publishing Corp.
All rights reserved. Used by permission.

Dear Reader:

We would appreciate hearing from you regarding the Rhapsody Romance series. It will enable us to continue to give you the best in inspirational romance fiction.

Mail to: Rhapsody Romance Editors
Harvest House Publishers, 1075 Arrowsmith, Eugene, OR 97402

1. What most influenced you to purchase **THE TENDER MELODY**?

   ☐ The Christian Story   ☐ Recommendations
   ☐ Cover   ☐ Other Rhapsody
   ☐ Backcover copy   Romances you've read
   ☐ _____

2. Your overall rating of this book:
   ☐ Excellent   ☐ Very good   ☐ Good   ☐ Fair   ☐ Poor

3. Which elements did you find most appealing in this book?
   ☐ Heroine   ☐ Story line
   ☐ Hero   ☐ Love Scenes
   ☐ Setting   ☐ Christian message

4. How many Rhapsody Romances have you read all together?
   (Choose one)   ☐ 1-2   ☐ 3-6   ☐ 7-10   ☐ Over 11

5. How likely would you be to purchase other Rhapsody Romances?
   ☐ Very likely   ☐ Not very likely
   ☐ Somewhat likely   ☐ Not at all

6. Please check the box next to your age group.
   ☐ Under 18   ☐ 25-34   ☐ 50-54
   ☐ 18-24   ☐ 35-39   ☐ Over 55

Name _____

Address _____

City _____ State _____ Zip _____

Rhapsody Romances

- [ ] **Another Love**, Joan Winmill Brown   3906
- [ ] **The Candy Shoppe**, Dorothy Abel   3884
- [ ] **The Heart That Lingers**, June Masters Bacher   3981
- [ ] **Love's Tender Voyage**, Joan Winmill Brown   3957
- [ ] **Promise Me Forever**, Colette Collins   3973
- [ ] **The Whisper of Love**, Dorothy Abel   3965
- [ ] **If Love Be Ours**, Joan Winmill Brown   4139
- [ ] **One True Love**, Arlene Cook   4163
- [ ] **Reflection of Love**, Susan Feldhake   4201
- [ ] **Until Then**, Dorothy Abel   4171
- [ ] **Until There Was You**, June Masters Bacher   4198
- [ ] **With All My Heart**, June Masters Bacher   4104
- [ ] **Forever Yours**, Arlene Cook   4383
- [ ] **Let Me Love Again**, Joan Winmill Brown   4392
- [ ] **My Heart To Give**, Carmen Leigh   4368
- [ ] **The Tender Melody**, Dorothy Abel   4287
- [ ] **Touched By Diamonds**, Colette Collins   4279
- [ ] **When Love Shines Through**, June Masters Bacher   4309

$2.95 each

At your local bookstore or use this handy coupon for ordering.

HARVEST HOUSE PUBLISHERS
1075 ARRROWSMITH, EUGENE, OREGON 97402

Please send me the book(s) I have checked above. I am enclosing $_____ (please add 50¢ per copy to cover postage and handling). Send check or money order—no cash or C.O.Ds. Please allow four weeks for delivery.

Name _____

Address _____

City _____ State _____ Zip _____

Phone _____